THE OBSIDIAN SISTERHOOD

1

A WEB OF OBSIDIAN

LYDIA M. HAWKE

**Published by Michem Publishing,
Canada**

This is a work of fiction. Names, characters, places, and incidents either are the sole product of the author's imagination or are used fictitiously, and any resemblance to actual persons, living or dead, business establishments, events, or locales is entirely coincidental.

A Web of Obsidian

February 25, 2025
Copyright © 2025 by Linda Poitevin

Cover design by Deranged Doctor Design
Interior design by AuthorTree

ISBN: 978-1-989457-28-3
MICHEM PUBLISHING

Dedicated to the memory of Samantha (@nobadcats on Twitter), who loved my books but couldn't stay to finish them. "Sweet fancy Moses in a muffin tin" belonged to her.

CHAPTER 1

"Well, fuck," I muttered. I stared at the neatly penciled columns of figures in the accounts book spread before me, my gaze resting on the last number in the last column of the last row. The very negative number. Then it lifted to the stack of envelopes sitting unopened by the desk lamp, the top one stamped with a bright red *OVERDUE*.

Then, because there didn't seem to be a better word for the kind of trouble the Mary Magdalene House for Women was in right now, I said it again, "Fuck, fuck, *fuck*."

Resting my elbows on the desk, I pinched the bridge of my nose beneath my glasses. I squeezed my eyes shut against the images my brain had insisted on conjuring all morning because the accounts themselves weren't stressful enough. Images of what would happen to the shelter's residents if we had to close.

Small, vulnerable Phoenix, with her spiky blond hair and brand-new lip piercing, back on the street without access to her hormone therapy; tall, stoic Therese returning to the man responsible for her horrific scars—and to almost-certain death; purple-haired Danelle turning tricks by night and carving her self-hatred into her skin by day; gruff Alice descending back into the drugs she'd fought so hard to leave behind ...

My eyes shot open, because closed they were just making my imaginings more vivid, and I stared again at the ledger. The numbers sat on the page, unflinching, unchanging, uncaring. I swore at them, too.

"Bloody, fucking *hell*," I growled. A corner of my mind winced at the language that was, at least in part, to blame for me having been thrown out of the convent—and the church I had once vowed to serve—more than twenty years before. But a greater part of me didn't … well, give a fuck, to be frank, because to my mind, my service had always been to a far greater power than an institution.

Especially a backward, man-made institution that had vetoed the idea of opening a shelter like the Mary Magdalene because it frowned upon the women I wanted to care for.

Because fuck that, too.

I winced again. My language had become a little over the top these days, even for me. I really should try to curtail it, if only for Sister Ernestine's sake. Her own tended toward the salty side, but she wasn't as likely as I was to slip up in front of the bishop, and while I might not officially be a nun anymore, watching my tongue seemed the least I could do as a boarder of the Sisters of St. Mary. Especially when they had folded me into their little family with such open-hearted welcome.

And when it had been Sister Ernestine herself who had assured me at my boarder suitability interview that, regardless of what the church might think, I was still—and always would be—a nun.

"As far as I can tell, Sister *Monica,"* she'd said, standing up from behind her desk and stretching her hand across to shake mine, *"your vows are intact. At least the ones that matter in this house."*

For all of that and more, it behooved me to at least try to clean up my language a little bit. But maybe I'd wait until after this particular crisis was over, because …

"Fuck," I growled again, as I returned to thinking about said crisis.

I slanted a look at the portrait of the shelter's namesake, hanging on the opposite wall, where it covered a hole in the plaster that had needed repair for as long as I could remember. Mary Magdalene gazed back, her expression implacable and not at all helpful.

I scowled at her, then leaned back in my chair and stared at the stained ceiling, also in need of repair. The shelter had never been profitable—that wasn't its purpose—but neither had it been quite this far in the hole before, with so few prospects for digging itself out. It was barely the end of summer, with more months than I cared to count before year end, when the annual donations turned over again. I'd already exhausted every ounce of goodwill my connections were willing to extend to one small shelter in the vast city of Toronto.

I threw the pencil I'd been using onto the desk and watched it skate across and drop off the other side. Scratch the *few* prospects idea. I had no prospects at all. I met Mary Magdalene's serene gaze again.

"You *could* do something other than just watch, you know," I told our patron sourly. Then I sighed. "I'm sorry. I know you do your best, and I *am* grateful. But we really could use your help right now, my friend. A way to cut back, a way to bring in more … something … anything?"

There was no response, of course. There never was, and I would be the first to run for help if I ever did receive an answer. I wholly believed in the power I served and the saint who watched over us, but I was far too much of a realist to think either would actually speak to me—or to anyone, for that matter. Pope included.

Which had been another reason for my "departure" from the church.

Ask me if I cared about that, either.

I pressed my lips together and returned my thoughts to the overwhelming problem at hand and my waning hope that I could keep the shelter afloat—or my momentum going. At the ripe old age of sixty-nine and counting, I was all too aware that my work in the neighborhood wasn't getting any easier.

That didn't, however, make it any less needed.

The clank of dishes and a muffled burst of laughter reached me through the swinging door that separated the kitchen from my office—formerly a butler's pantry in the shelter's days as a much grander house. Despite the certain financial doom looming over us, I smiled. Lunchtime, I thought, glancing at the digital clock sitting on the corner of my desk.

Tonya, self-appointed chief cook, had promised gazpacho today because it was too hot to cook in the un-airconditioned house. It would be the fourth time the residents had all sat down together at the battered harvest table they'd lugged home last week from an alley three blocks away. And yes, I was still counting, because each of the occasions was worth marking.

The thing was massive. It had taken their combined strength and strategy to maneuver it up the back steps and into the kitchen—and another team effort to clean it of decades of grunge—but it had been worth the struggle. For the first time in the shelter's twenty-year history, all of its residents had eaten at the same table at the same time, further cementing the bonds that had drawn them together. Ties stronger by far than family ones, even though the faces had changed so many times over the years.

I pushed back from the desk, my gaze going one last time to the accounts book and its negative balance as I stood. Some days, I couldn't help but think how things might have been different if I'd found a way to stay within the church. If I'd requested a transfer away from St. Paul's Monastery to another, more accepting, convent. If I'd been compliant enough to remain part of the fold. Then, perhaps, I might have at least been able to ask for an emergency loan.

My mouth twisted. Except all of this—the shelter, our independence, the women who gathered together for lunch in the kitchen beyond—only existed because I *had* broken away. Because I'd already spent twenty-five years thinking I could change things from within the institution, and I had achieved exactly nothing. Because I'd been so bitter and disillusioned and angry that I could see only one way out for myself, and Mother Annunciata and Archbishop Grant had agreed—and sped me on my way.

Because, when it came down to it, I could not remain part of a system that turned its back on the diversity that was simple human nature, genetics, science. Just as my father had turned his back on one of his own.

I slammed the ledger shut, and my gaze went to the words that I'd had tattooed on the back of my left hand in celebration of opening the shelter. NO REGRETS, it reminded me, and I squared my shoulders and lifted my chin. It didn't matter if I was sixty-nine or a hundred and nine. As long as I had breath left in my body, I would find a way to keep the shelter going, and to ensure that its residents were safe and fed and—

A shriek pierced the air, and I forgot about breathing altogether as my head snapped up and my gaze locked on the door. That had sounded like—

The shriek came again, and I bolted for the kitchen.

CHAPTER 2

A HALF-DOZEN WIDE-EYED GAZES LOCKED ONTO ME AS I burst through the door. Before I could even begin a head-count, spiky-haired Phoenix pointed toward the door leading to the hallway and the front of the house.

"It's Cindy," she said. "She went to get the—"

Another screech cut her off.

With my entire flock on my heels, I ran from the kitchen. Cindy Blackwater stood in the front doorway, filling her lungs for another go at yelling when I reached her. The young woman jumped when I put a hand on her shoulder, and huge, dark eyes looked up, filled with horror. She launched herself into my arms.

"She's dead she's dead she's dead!" The words ran together as she buried her face in my shoulder, her voice muffled. "I know she's dead!"

I gave the young woman's head a hasty pat and pried her arms loose, then passed her to Alice, who in turn shuffled her along to the rest of the group. For an instant, Alice's grim gaze met mine. We'd had our fair share of injured and/or otherwise damaged women show up on our porch, but a body?

In the shelter's entire twenty-year history, that would be a first.

I took a deep breath and stepped onto the porch. A pile of rags lay at the top of the stairs, with skeletal limbs sticking out from it, all akimbo, draped in loose, paper-thin skin. None of the limbs moved.

My heart dropped and my belly churned. Dear sweet Mary, that did not look good. The bones at the top of the stairs twitched and a tiny mewling sound emerged from them.

"Holy Mother," I muttered.

"Jesus," Alice concurred. She shouldered past me to kneel beside the bones. "It's alive."

Not he. Not she. Not even a neutral *they*.

It.

Because while Cindy had said *she*, there seemed no way to be sure, and in this state, it looked more creature than human. And Alice was right. *It* was alive. But not by much.

I pressed my lips together and raked my gaze over the women crowded in the doorway behind us. Some looked anxious, others curious; a couple showed serious signs of being triggered by the events. There would be psychological fallout from this, but that would have to wait. First, we had a life to save. I hoped.

I focused on the tallest figure at the back, a stoic, scarred woman who had been at the shelter for almost two years, and who had graduated from resident to my first full-time staff member last month—a position that would be short-lived if I didn't find some funding soon. But that was a worry for later. I pointed at the woman.

"Therese, call 911 and tell them we need an ambulance and—" I hesitated, glancing back at the kneeling Alice. Given the background of some of the women living here, we tried our best to avoid a police presence in the home, but in a situation such as this, we had no choice. I looked at Therese again.

"And the police," I finished firmly.

As one of the residents who had little reason to trust cops, Therese scowled, but she nodded and disappeared back into the house, and I turned to join Alice.

Dropping to my knees on the top step of the porch, beside the figure, I smoothed back matted, chin-length hair streaked with gray, My fingers brushed the forehead beneath. There was no response, and there had been no further sound.

Jaw tight, I met Alice's gaze across the potential corpse. "Well?"

Alice shrugged. "She's breathing," she muttered, "but barely."

"What can I do?"

"Unless you can conjure a miracle," the other woman growled, "not much." She sat back on her heels, her expression equal parts angry and helpless, her hands resting on her stout thighs. "I doubt she'll last until the paramedics get here."

"Can she be moved?"

Once, in a long-ago former lifetime that Alice didn't often talk about, she had been a registered nurse, making her far better qualified than I was to assess the damage. Her response wasn't promising.

"I don't think it will matter either way," she said, her voice quiet.

I pressed my lips together and made a decision. "Well, then, we're not letting her die on the porch."

Before she could object, I shifted to one knee and braced my other foot beneath me, then slid my arms under the wasted body. My heart lurched at the feel of bones resting in my hands, but I pushed aside my horror and rose to my feet. Even if I hadn't been in better than average shape for my sixty-nine years, there was so little to the woman I lifted that I hardly noticed her weight.

The stench rising from her, however, was another story —and enough to knock an elephant to its knees.

"Jesus Christ," Tonya mumbled from behind the hand she'd slapped over her mouth and nose. "You *sure* she's not already dead?"

The woman made another faint, piteous mewl in response.

I turned her head to the side, swallowing hard and blinking back the haze of tears brought on by both heartbreak and odor. Breathing shallowly through my mouth and keeping my head tilted as far away as my neck would allow, I headed into the house. The cluster of women gave way before me, then trailed behind, a couple of them gagging at the smell.

"Wait!" Alice pushed past me into the TV room and grabbed a blanket off the back of a chair. She spread it over the couch. "Put her on that," she directed. "Otherwise, we'll have to pitch the entire couch onto the street. Therese! Where's the damned ambulance?"

"They said at least ten minutes," responded the tall woman, who had rejoined the group. Her voice was roughened by decades of smoking and the bronchial infections that plagued her. "But the police—"

"Can't do a bloody thing," Alice growled as I settled my bundle gently on the couch.

I reached for the blanket edges to tuck them around the woman, but Alice's hand stopped me. She shrugged when I looked up at her.

"Just because I don't think she'll make it doesn't mean I can't try."

I nodded and stepped back from the stinking skeleton —a little too gratefully, I thought with a stab of guilt—to let her take over. Alice's thick fingers searched for a pulse at the side of the emaciated throat, and a small breath of relief escaped her.

"Right," she said. "I'll have to take her clothes off to examine her, so I need scissors and a bag of some kind."

"A bag?"

"For evidence."

I glanced at the dark stain across the front of the woman's shirt. The question wasn't *if* it was blood, but who the blood belonged to. "Of course," I responded. I unclipped a ring of keys from my belt loop and held them out to one of the other women. "Danelle?"

Sloe-eyed and silent, Danelle warily eyed the offering. She was the reason the scissors and knives were kept in a locked drawer in the kitchen, along with any other sharp instruments that might be used to add to the scars that crisscrossed her arms, legs, and belly. In the six months she'd been at the shelter, she had never been entrusted with the means to access them unsupervised. Now, with another's life for her to focus on, was as good a time as any to change that.

Danelle, however, made no move to take the keys.

"Do you want me to send someone else?" I asked.

She hesitated, then shook her purple-dyed head. She reached out a thin arm, its sleeve past her wrist even in the heatwave gripping the city, and took the keys. I held onto them for a fraction of an instant, folding both my hands around hers.

"Be quick," I whispered. She lifted her chin a fraction and nodded, then turned to slip past Tonya, who had returned with a bowl of water and a stack of threadbare towels.

Alice motioned for the bowl to go on the coffee table beside her. She dipped the corner of a towel into it and squeezed out the excess water, shooting a dark, sidelong look at me. "You sure that was smart? I don't need to be patching her up, too."

"She'll be fine," I said.

Grunting, Alice turned to sponge the woman's face, exposing bruises and infected scrapes and scratches.

Alice inhaled sharply. "Fucking hell. She's older than I thought she was. Much."

"Elder abuse?" Nausea churned in my belly.

The former nurse didn't answer me. She didn't have to. She sucked in a lungful of air instead and bellowed, "Danelle! Where are my damned scissors?"

"She only just—" I began, but a scurry of footsteps cut my words short. Danelle scooted back into the room, scissors and paper grocery bag in hand. She held them out to Alice and received another grunt in return, then handed me the key ring and melted back into the cluster of women around the couch. At the back of the group, Therese disappeared out the door into the hallway.

Alice began cutting away the woman's clothing, beginning with the hem of what was left of her t-shirt. I hovered nearby, wanting to help but not wanting to interfere as she peeled back the shirt to either side. Beneath it, crusted blood and dirt covered the woman's skin so thickly, it looked as if it had become part of her. As if there was no way to tell where human ended and dirt—or whatever else caused that stench—began.

"Fucking hell," Alice muttered again. "She's so filthy, I can't see anything."

"That blood on her dress hadda come from somewhere," Lissa pointed out.

Alice slanted her an impatient look. "You think, genius?"

Lissa muttered something under her breath, and Tonya gave her a hard nudge in the ribs. Before I could open my mouth to say anything, Therese returned to the room, shouldering between the two women and sending each of them a dark, quelling look as she clipped her own key ring back onto her belt.

I exchanged a quick look with her, and she inclined her

head once, almost imperceptibly—confirmation that a successful kitchen utensil count had been undertaken. I breathed a small sigh of relief …

And then the screaming started.

IT TOOK ME A MOMENT TO IDENTIFY THE SOURCE OF THE screams. Another to convince myself to peel my hands away from my ears, where I'd slapped them in a futile effort to mute the sound—or at least muffle it. Because the screams—no, the scream, singular, because it seemed unending—was that high. That piercing. That deafening.

Chaos erupted around me as the shelter residents pressed fingers into their own ears and shouted at Alice to make the woman stop. But Alice, too, had retreated from the sound.

Gritting my teeth, I dived toward the couch and its occupant. The woman's eyes—a flat, dead brown—were open and staring at the ceiling. There was nothing behind them. No awareness. No presence. The screaming continued.

Trying to keep my touch gentle despite the pain in my ears and my borderline desperation, I gripped the skeletal shoulders and shook her. It had no effect. The unending scream became hoarse but continued, grating against my every fiber. My grip on the shoulders tightened, and I forced myself to let go and step away from the urge to do something—anything—to stop the horrific, heartrending, eardrum-shattering noise. My hands went back to my ears.

"Sister!"

A shoulder bumped against my arm, and I turned my

head to find Lissa, fingers still in her ears, standing beside me.

"We have company!" the woman yelled, jerking an elbow toward the front-room window.

"Police?" I yelled back.

Lissa shook her head. "Ain't no cop I know carries a crowbar."

"Shit," I muttered. I stared at the woman on the sofa, my hands curling into fists but for the index fingers poked inside my ear canals. It wouldn't be the first time someone had followed his prey to our doorstep. It might, however, be the first time I wanted to do more than hold him off until the cops arrived. My fists tightened. The woman screamed on.

I looked at Lissa standing watch at the window, then toward the doorway. Only Alice, Phoenix and Therese remained, their expressions both pained and determined as they gazed back at me for guidance, trusting my judgment.

Trusting me to keep them safe.

Quickly, efficiently, I sorted through my options. They weren't many. If I stayed in the house, the crowbar would make short shrift of the living room window, and the man would be inside with all of us within seconds. If I went out to him, he would have to go through me to get to the window, which would at least buy a few extra minutes for help to arrive. I took a deep breath and plucked my fingertips from my ears, then grabbed Alice's arm. I pushed the former nurse toward the woman on the sofa.

"Do what you can to keep her alive," I shouted. "Therese, call the police again, and tell them we have an armed intruder. Phoenix, keep the others in the kitchen."

"I'll come—" Therese began.

"No," I said. "Stay here. No one comes outside until I know what's going on."

Chapter 3

Blissful semi-silence enveloped me as I stepped onto the porch and closed the door behind me, shutting off the screams. My eyes wanted to close in involuntary relief, but I had no time to enjoy the respite. Not when my gaze landed on a solitary man on the sidewalk side of the rickety picket fence separating the shelter from the busy street beyond.

I sized him up, weighing my chances if my efforts to dissuade him with words failed. Thickly built and on the shorter side—maybe five foot six or seven—he had short-cropped sandy hair and was dressed all in black. Black jeans, a black turtleneck, black leather gloves, black sunglasses. Everything but the latter was out of keeping with the unseasonably sweltering early September afternoon.

And Lissa had been right: he carried a crowbar.

Two decades of martial arts and two black belts aside, *that* might pose a problem.

I tried to meet his gaze, but his eyes were invisible behind the sunglasses, and uneasiness trickled down my spine. An electric streetcar rolled past behind him, its trolley poles clattering over a junction in the wires feeding it. A cicada buzzed somewhere in the tree beside the apartment building next door. A siren wailed in the distance, too far away to be helpful anytime soon, assuming that it was even headed to us.

Over by the gate, the man smiled—cold, cocky, utterly certain of himself. Like most people, he saw no threat in a getting-on-in-years, gray-haired woman. I held back a grim smile of my own, because, like most people, he would be mistaken.

I walked across the porch toward the stairs, automatically tugging my blouse free of my waistband and undoing the buttons at each cuff. The first rule of every martial art I'd ever studied was to avoid engaging in a fight, but the second was to be ready if one came.

The door behind me opened, and I glanced back long enough to see some of the residents crowded into the doorway. Briefly, I noted that the screams in the house had stopped, but I didn't have time to dwell on why. I returned my gaze to the man in time to see him push the sleeves of his turtleneck back from muscled forearms. The action was too deliberate to be casual, and when I saw the exposed tattoo on the inside of his right arm, I knew why.

The frisson of unease between my shoulder blades turned to a slither of foreboding. A trickle of sweat joined it. I slipped the pendant I wore—a Mary Magdalene medallion—over my head and laid it on the porch rail.

"Get back inside," I told the women over my shoulder. "All of you. Let me handle this."

If I did have to get into it with our uninvited guest, I didn't need to be worrying about who might get in the way —and who might get hurt in addition to me.

"But, Sister—"

"You can't stay out here by yourself—"

"We're not leaving you alone!"

The simultaneous chorus of objections ran together into a blur of voices, but they ground to a halt when I held up a hand.

"Inside," I repeated. "Please. I'll be fine. I'm just going to keep him busy until the police get here. The best thing you can do is call *them* again."

Footsteps sounded, approaching rather than retreating,

and then Therese was at my side, leaning in to mutter, "That tattoo on his arm is gang. You don't want to mess with him."

"I know what it is." I'd seen the tattoo many times before in the neighborhood, and I knew exactly what it meant ... and that the *gang* Therese spoke of was nothing less than the Russian mob.

Hey, Mary Magdalene? If you're listening, I could use those cops soon.

The man reached the tattooed arm over the crooked, metal-framed wire gate and unlatched it. Beside me, Therese scowled and crossed her arms.

"Well," she said, "then you should also know there's no way in hell we're leaving you out here by your—"

A new scream from inside the house cut her off. The man had stepped through the gate, and the instant his foot touched the path inside the yard, the gut-piercing, eardrum-perforating screech started up again, going on and on and on. I scrunched my eyes shut against its awfulness, but sudden caution whispered through my belly, and they snapped open again almost instantly.

Shock jolted through me. I'd barely blinked, and the man was already halfway across the front yard, crowbar swinging at his side. I inhaled a sharp breath. Sweet Mary, he'd moved fast. Too fast for me to pretend that this wasn't going to get ugly before help arrived.

I gritted my teeth and looked around the worn porch that was as desperately in need of a coat of paint as the rest of the house. My gaze fell on a broom propped against the pillar on the other side of the stairs. It wasn't much, but it would have to do.

I shoved Therese toward the door and raised my voice over the woman's screech. I did not, however, take my eyes off my opponent again.

I didn't dare.

"Inside," I snapped at the women. "All of you. Lissa, help Alice. Therese, call the police again and see how far away they are. Tonya, come back and tell me, but do *not* step out of that house. Is that clear?"

Tell me so I'll know how long I have to hold out.

"But, Sister—" Lissa began.

"*Go*," I barked.

I didn't—couldn't—hear them leave, but there were no more objections, and an emptiness at my back told me that the women had withdrawn. I took a deep, steadying breath and flexed my fingers. I wasn't looking forward to this next part. Not even a little bit.

I crossed the porch to stand at the top of the stairs beside the broom and drew myself up to my full five-foot, four-inch height. At least in that respect, my opponent and I were reasonably well matched, I thought darkly. I settled my sneaker-clad feet against the porch floorboards, finding my center. Grounding myself.

Traffic streamed by on the street beyond the yard, and a heavily muscled man strode past on the sidewalk with a small dog clutched in his arms, casting alarmed glances at me and the crowbar-wielding man. He didn't stop.

No one in this neighborhood stopped for trouble anymore. It was, in large part, why the neighborhood had become what it was in the first place. That, and the increasing reluctance of the police to bother with us.

But those were problems for another day.

"That's far enough," I shouted. "The police are on their way, and—"

I stopped as the man raised his free hand and snapped finger against thumb, and the scream from inside the house abruptly cut off. The man slid the sunglasses he wore onto the top of his head. Gray eyes regarded me with a flat iciness at odds with the faint smile playing across his lips.

"Much better," he said. "You were saying?"

But before I could respond, more yelling came from the house. Distinctly alarmed yelling. I sifted rapidly through the voices—Alice's, bellowing for help; Danelle's, her screams replacing the woman's, albeit not as loud; Lissa yelling at Danelle—with no effect—to shut the fuck up.

My focus on the danger facing me wavered. What in the name of Mary herself—

"Sister!" Tonya yelled behind me.

So much yelling.

I looked over my shoulder to find her in the doorway, her face white and eyes frantic, her hands cupped around her mouth in a makeshift megaphone.

"Ten minutes, Sister!" she called. "The fucking cops said *another* ten minutes! And the woman—she's having a seizure or something!"

My breath caught, and I hesitated. Another ten minutes? Holy Mother, where were they coming from? The other side of the city? I hadn't even engaged with my opponent yet, and I already doubted my ability to keep him at bay that long. Maybe I should just go back into the house and barricade the—

I turned back to the man and my stomach lurched. He'd crossed half the remaining yard and stood a mere six feet away from the stairs. How—?

I cut the thought short. How didn't matter. Making sure he didn't get any closer did. I was seriously rethinking my decision to leave the house, but it was too late for that. There was no way I could get back inside and lock the temperamental deadbolt before he got to me. Like it or not, I was going to have to stand my ground.

No regrets.

Calm descended with the decision, the kind of calm that came with decades of training and brought clarity in its wake. Holding my opponent's gaze unflinchingly, I reached for the broom, braced it against the porch floor, and brought one foot down on the handle, just above the bristles. The broomstick snapped with a loud crack, and I kicked the bristles aside. Then I gripped my makeshift stick with both hands and held it across my body.

"I *said* that's far enough," I repeated. "You need to leave."

The man swung the crowbar in a lazy circle at his side. He shrugged. "I'd like to, but I can't. Not without what I came for."

"And I can't let you take her."

He snorted. "Her? You can keep *her*. I want only what she has with her. Then I'll go."

He spoke with no accent, and his diction told me he was well educated. If he *was* mob, he wasn't their usual recruit. I filed away the details for my police statement.

I wondered what the woman might have taken from him—and where on her person, amid those filthy rags, she could possibly have hidden it. I turned my head a fraction, so that I could see the doorway from the corner of my eye while still keeping my gaze firmly on the man, thinking to send Tonya to find out. But the other woman was gone again.

My grip firm on the broomstick, I descended the stairs —four of them—to stand at their base. A scant few feet separated us now.

"Look," I said. "We don't want any trouble. The police are on their way, but if you leave now—"

The man lunged, and the crowbar came at my head with a speed that required the skill and agility of every single one of my twenty-one years of training and both black belts to avoid. I pivoted away on pure instinct, striking out with my broomstick at the backs of my opponent's knees as I slid past and dropped into a defensive stance halfway across the lawn, well out of his reach. My scalp tingled with the sensation of metal brushing against my hair, and shock and adrenaline flooded my veins. Holy Mother, this man was not fooling around.

My opponent had replaced me at the foot of the stairs, seemingly uninjured by the blow I'd delivered, even though my hand still tingled from the impact of broomstick against leg. His gaze narrowed in assessment, however, and he glanced between me and the porch, seeming to weigh his chances of getting to his prey before I could interfere.

Good. That meant I hadn't been the only one surprised by our initial clash, but how had he moved so fast? And how in heaven's name was he still standing after that whack I'd landed?

Never mind, I told myself. *Just stay focused and keep him occupied long enough for the police to get here.*

I settled one end of the broomstick against the concrete path and again brought my foot down on it, snapping it into two pieces, one for each hand. They would be no match for the metal crowbar itself, but stick work was one of my strongest skill sets, and they'd be enough to break a hand or numb a limb if I could get past said crowbar. At least, they should be.

Ignoring the feather of doubt brushing against my mind, I held the sticks wide, vying for time.

"You still have time to leave," I said. "We don't have to do—"

Again with no warning, no tell of any kind, the man lunged at me. Again I reacted instinctively, stepping back from the attack and twisting out of the way. But this time I wasn't fast enough, and the crowbar glanced off my shoulder, sending a crippling shock of pain down my arm. My hand went numb, and only sheer determination kept me from dropping the stick.

The caution that had stirred in me at the man's arrival thickened into uncertainty tinged with fear.

In all my years of sparring and my many street fights, I had never seen anyone move this fast. Or with such precision. This was no ordinary gang member I fought.

He's no ordinary man at all, something whispered inside me. *There's something wrong with him. Something—*

Before the thought could complete itself, my opponent came at me again. I deflected the crowbar away from my skull, but its impact tore the makeshift weapon from my already-numbed grasp and sent it spiraling through the air and into the overgrown rosebush at the end of the porch. This time, however, I didn't step away.

Instead I, too, lunged, swinging the remaining stick in a sideways arc aimed at the man's ribs. It connected full on … and shattered on impact.

A dozen splinters dropped to the uneven grass, leaving me stunned and unarmed—and leaving my opponent as unperturbed as if I'd hit him with a feather duster. I backed away, acutely conscious of my vulnerability. Over-whelmingly aware that there were still no sirens.

White teeth flashed in the sunlight as the man smirked, then chuckled. He sauntered toward me, taking one step for every two that I took, gripping his weapon with both hands and resting it against his shoulder like he might a baseball bat. His gray eyes stared into mine, devoid of emotion. Devoid of light.

"I win," he said.

And then he swung.

Chapter 4

I DIVED ASIDE AND DROPPED INTO A ROLL TO EVADE THE blow, but I didn't make it. Metal smashed into my shoulder blade, and I felt bone give way beneath it. Stars exploded behind my eyeballs. Agony cascaded through my body.

Biting back a screech, I fought off the darkness encroaching at the edges of consciousness. *Move*, my inner voice urged. *Move now or you die*.

I groaned as I staggered upright and turned to face my opponent, one arm hanging uselessly at my side. Again, the crowbar smashed into me.

This time, the blow connected with my rib cage and lifted me from my feet. I sailed through the air to land amid the dandelions scattered across the lawn. My shattered shoulder took the brunt of the landing, and for a moment, time stood utterly still as the world spun on its axis and my whole being refused to function. Somewhere in the back of my mind, the beginnings of a prayer hovered, but it died unformed as the man across the lawn came back into focus.

He stood with legs splayed and weapon dangling at his side. Expression glittered in his gray eyes now. Rage and hatred and—my heart did a flip in my chest. *Emptiness*, I thought. The kind of emptiness that bred contempt and pure, unadulterated evil. That could take a life—my life— and not even blink.

In the space of a single heartbeat, I knew that he was right. He'd won. I'd done my best to keep him from the woman, but the sirens I could finally hear wailing their approach wouldn't reach us in time.

This was it, I thought with no small amount of surprise. There would be no miracle. No divine intervention. I had—without fanfare or fuss of any kind—simply come to the end of my journey, and I was going to die, here on the lawn of the center I had founded to protect women. Even in the haze of shock that dulled every sense, the irony in that did not escape me.

As if he'd read my thoughts, the man bared his teeth in a bizarre kind of smile and began a slow stalk toward me, his feet crushing the green blades of grass and the white clover blossoms that dotted the lawn. A bumblebee drifted up and away from his encroachment, its body heavy with pollen. A crow on the wires above the sidewalk cawed harshly.

The slow calm of acceptance descended. I turned my head away from my attacker and closed my eyes. I would not watch death approach, I decided. Nor would I give him the satisfaction of seeing my pain. Instead, I would pray. I would pray as I always did in times of trouble. Not as I had been trained to pray, but as I had learned to do despite that training.

I would pray for the lives of others. Those of the passersby who didn't stop to help, for the women inside the house and the one we had tried to shelter, for the women who would now never find their way here, for the sisters I would leave—

"Sister Monica!" a woman's voice called. I didn't recognize it, and even if I had, I would still have ignored it. I had a lot to say to my Mother and limited time to say it before my opponent struck the killing blow, and—

"Sister Monica!" the voice called again. It came from the direction of the house, as rasping as it was unfamiliar, and compelling in a way that made my thoughts pause. Despite my need to call the right words to me in this, the last of my time here on Earth, I opened my eyes and twisted my head toward the house. Slowly, the stairs came into focus … and then the porch … and then the figure standing at the edge of it.

Skeleton woman had emerged from the house and stood clutching one of the posts, swaying on her feet. She looked too fragile even to stand, but somehow, she still gave the impression of strength and grace, and her expression radiated calm command. She raised a shaking hand, and something glinted dully in her grasp.

"This is yours now," she said. "Find the others."

With surprising strength, she tossed the object high, and it sailed through the air across the lawn. But my attention was focused not on it—nor the woman who'd thrown it. It was on my opponent.

The brutal, black-clad man whose gaze had left me and who now tracked the object with an avarice that took away what little breath remained in my struggling lungs. An avarice that pierced me to my core and spawned an absolute, utter, icy certainty in me that, under no circumstances, could he be allowed to have it.

It took a split second to make the decision. Another to thrust my good arm between my chest and the grass, push up onto my knees, and rock back on my heels. A third to heave myself to my feet through the agony that tried to paralyze me. Then, as the object began its graceful, arcing descent, I launched myself toward it with all the strength and every atom of willpower that I possessed.

My body slammed into my opponent's as he reached for the object arcing toward him. He staggered under the impact, knocked just enough off balance that his gloved fingers closed on empty air.

Mine, however, snagged the object in mid-flight.

I tucked it against my chest and curled into a roll I'd practiced so many times that it had become second nature. A roll intended to protect me from injury—except it was far too late for that. Broken bone ends ground together, already traumatized tissues shredded further, and I fell face first into the grass in a cloud of agony. Tears flooded my eyes, and the air left my lungs in a garbled whimper and refused to return.

Through the haze of pain enveloping me, I braced for the crowbar's inevitable impact. Long, excruciating seconds slid by. Then more. But no blow came.

The haze began to lift, allowing coherent thought to filter back. I drew a tiny, cautious breath and slowly, carefully, lifted my head and brought the world back into focus.

The man stood a dozen feet away, scowling with a malevolence that made me flinch. For an instant, the ice water of panic flooded my belly. I didn't know where I'd found the reserves to tackle him that last time, but I was absolutely and utterly certain that I could not do it again. Hell, I had no idea why I'd done so in the first place—and where in the name of heaven itself were those cops? The sirens had stopped again, and I could hear nothing from the house or the women inside it, and—

The man shifted his grip on the crowbar, and I cringed. But he made no move toward me. No move at all except to flail his arms as if fighting for his balance as his expression flickered between bafflement and …

I blinked. Fear? No, that couldn't be right, because surely he could see that I was done. That I couldn't so much as stand, never mind repeat the impossible feat I'd pulled off moments ago.

My injuries were muddling my thoughts, and I wanted to shake my head to clear it, but I didn't dare. Didn't—

Forgetting all about the agony that encased my lungs, I drew a sharp, startled breath as the man shrieked in terror and flailed again. He struggled to lift one foot and then the other, but both stayed rooted to the ground, and—

The fear that drove him stirred in me, too, as the lawn between us began to writhe as if something moved beneath it. Something long and narrow and—

Sweet holy Mother of All, what the *fuck* was that?

Shock jolted me upright—or would have, if my hand hadn't been as stuck to the lawn as the man's feet appeared to be. I stared at my outstretched arm and the tightly curled fingers clenched into a fist at the end of it. At the hard black edges peeking out between thumb and forefinger. At the fine, silver strands wrapped around my fingers and the object inside them, tying me and it to the ground, and at the writhing beneath the grass that extended toward—

Horror filled me, and my gaze fastened again on the man struggling to pull his feet free of the lawn—no, not the lawn. I could see them now. The same silver threads that wrapped my fist had encased his feet and were climbing his legs, twisting around his torso, reaching for his arms, his throat, the mouth that had opened in a wide, silent scream ...

And then the fire started.

My eyes snapped back to my hand as the object I clutched grew hot, then hotter, then scorching. I gasped and tried to uncurl my fingers and fling it away, but the silver threads held fast. My horror gave way to fresh panic licking through my veins.

Except ... except it wasn't panic at all. It was heat. Heat from the damned whatever-it-was that I held, running through me from head to toe and back again, turning my insides—my bones, my organs, my everything —molten.

My eyes watered, and I looked across the twisting lawn to the man held as captive as I was. A gut-wrenching terror in the gaze that met mine begged for my help, but I didn't know how. *Pray*, I wanted to call to him, but I didn't have the strength, couldn't find my voice in a throat gone tight with my own fear.

Of all the ways I'd thought I might die, I could honestly say that the possibility of spontaneous combustion had never occurred to me. I searched within me for my previous calm, but the flames at my core had devoured it. All I had left was a return to my prayers—a call to my patron saint, my chosen protector, the woman whose teachings had resonated with me in ways that others had not.

Hail Mary Magdalene, full of grace, I thought, *come and sit with me.*

The object in my grasp began to throb with a strong, slow pulse like that of a heartbeat, and the fire consuming me from the inside blossomed, swelled, pushed against my margins.

Hail Mary Magdalene, sister to us all, come and pray for me ...

The cobwebs—for that was what they reminded me of —engulfed the man's face, obliterating his terror and swallowing his scream. He was entirely cocooned now, and silent.

Pray for him.

My gaze traveled slowly, painfully to the porch and the women clustered there, clinging to one another, incomprehension and grief in the eyes that stared back at me. The women I'd sworn to protect. The skeletal woman lying at their feet.

The edges of my consciousness began to fray.

"Pray for us all," I whispered.

The fire shot outward from me. With the last of my awareness, I watched the writhing grass become a spreading circle of dust that traveled toward the man. The cocoon encasing him burst into blue flames that flared high like a torch might …

And then he exploded, and my world went dark.

CHAPTER 5

I CAME TO ON A GURNEY.

For long, muddled minutes, I drifted in and out of awareness before I fully surfaced. I stared up at a disorienting array of too-bright lights as a crowd of people moved around me, shouting unintelligibly, distantly. Cool air rushed across my chest, and my bra gave way, spilling me to either side. Hands poked and prodded at my arms, my shoulders, my belly. I opened my mouth to object, but a flash of light across my eyes distracted me. Words filtered into my brain through the ringing in my skull, "*...awake ... CT scan ... full set ... X-rays ... blood type ...*"

None of them made sense, and I tried harder to focus. Something had happened. Something ... not good. I was —I had no idea where I was. Wait—did I know *who* I was? Panic tugged at the fringes of consciousness, and more words jumbled together. I tried to sort them out.

"*... holding something ... hand ... relax ... get it out ...*"

Fingers pried at my clenched right hand. I clutched harder and tried to turn my head to look, but something rigid around my neck held me immobile. The panic ramped up a notch, and I struggled for air. A face loomed above me, almost obscured by a low-riding cap, mask, and face shield. More words came from it.

"*... let go ... tests ... Monica ...*"

My entire focus zeroed in on the *Monica* as the fingers prying at my hand unfolded my thumb. That was it. That was me. I was Monica. Sister Monica. And in my hand was—

NO.

I tore away from the grip on my hand and surged up and off the gurney amid shouts of alarm. A man grabbed for me, and without thought—or even awareness—I evaded him and drove the heel of my other hand into his nose. Bone gave way beneath my blow, and he dropped like a—

Stone, I thought. *I have to protect the stone.*

Ducking away from the other hands reaching for me, I bolted from the room and fled into the corridor beyond. Someone behind me called for assistance. Someone else bellowed at me to stop. I ignored both, my entire being focused on the hard object in my palm and an exit sign at the end of the hall. Oblivious to the people scattering out of my path, I staggered toward it, tearing away the cervical collar around my neck and letting it drop to the floor. I didn't know where I was going—sweet Mary, I had no idea where I was in the first place—but I knew I had to get out of here. Had to get *it* out of here because I couldn't let anyone take it from me.

Overhead, an intercom crackled to life. *"Code white, emergency ward. Code white, emergency ward."*

A vague memory jogged in my brain. I knew those words … didn't I? My steps slowed, and I pressed my free hand to my temple. Fuck, but my head hurt.

"Code white, emergency ward," the intercom said again.

Three repetitions. Code white—a violent situation. Emergency …

I stopped and looked around myself. At the curtained cubicles; the handful of doors to more private rooms; the pale yellow walls and highly polished floor; the gurneys and wheelchairs lining the corridor; the wide, curving sweep of a nurse's station … the alarmed eyes of a mother carefully tucking her son behind her as she backed away—

From me. She was backing away from me, because—

I stared down at my bare chest and the heart monitor wires sprouting from the discs stuck to it, then at the blood trickling down my arm from the hand I'd put to my head. Slowly I lowered the hand again and stared at the dislodged IV needle dangling from it, held on by a strip of tape. My brain sputtered, trying to come online.

Hospital. I was in hospital. In the ER, to be more precise, and the code white was—

Two security guards burst through the swinging doors at the end of the corridor, grim, focused intent in their every tense line, and their eyes locked on—

Me again.

The air wheezed from my lungs. Me, because *I* was the violent situation. Surprise and understanding collided in my brain, and I held my hands up in a gesture of surrender.

"Wait," I said, shaking my head. "There's been a mistake. I'm not violent. I didn't mean to—"

Or at least, that was what I intended to do and say.

The reality, however, was a little different. And it was driven by the damnable stone that I held aloft and waved at the approaching guards. A stone whose webs—because it totally made sense that a stone should come with webs, right?—encased my hand and began crawling up (down?) my arm as visions of an exploding man danced across my brain and I screeched, "Stop! Stay back, or it will destroy you, too!"

They did stop, probably more out of surprise than fear of the crazy old lady brandishing a tiny rock at them, but the reason didn't matter. Getting out of here before they came at me again did. I might not know what the stone was, but I did know that there was no way in hell I would give it another chance to kill someone.

Before I could think better of my idea—which was

flawed at best—I turned tail and bolted for the other end of the corridor. Heart monitor wires flopped against my bare breasts, my breasts flopped against my rib cage, a part of me expressed surprise that said rib cage didn't hurt more after the crowbar beating it had taken, a larger part was dumbfounded that any of this was happening at all, and then someone tackled me from behind and my flight to freedom ended in a face plant and a skid across the floor.

As the light faded from my world for a second time, my last coherent—figuratively speaking—action was to thrust the smooth, fiery hot stone into the pocket of the jeans I still wore as I tried desperately to ignore the voice deep inside my mind that urged me to fight back.

And then to tell it to hush before someone heard it.

The second time I surfaced into consciousness, I was alone in a semi-darkened room and I felt like I'd been run over by a train.

Everything from my eyebrows to my toes hurt—and I couldn't even explore the pain because I was trussed up like a turkey and tied to the bed. I lay still for a moment—partly because of the restraints, partly because my head felt like it might explode if I moved it, but mostly because my entire being felt frozen—in time, in circumstance ... in a void I'd never encountered before. A confused loop of *what the fuck* traveled through my mind as I cautiously moved my eyes to scan what I could see of my surroundings.

It was enough to identify the room as being in a hospital, and that was enough to trigger a flood of memories. The what-the-fuck loop morphed into a stunned—and horrified—*oh, sweet Mary, what have I done?*

Slugging the nurse. Running half-naked down the

corridor. The attack on the lawn of the Mary Magdalene shelter.

The stone.

I sucked in a deep, ragged breath, regretted it when pain lanced through my ribcage—front and back—and lifted my head from the pillow. I regretted that, too, but grimly ignored the army of drummers beating on the inside of my skull as I twisted my head to the left, then the right. My gaze settled on a shadow across the room, and I made out a pile of clothing stacked on a chair. The stone was there. I was sure of it. I could—feel it?

I shivered beneath the thin blanket, and the shackled hand that had held the stone curled involuntarily into a fist beside me. In unspoken rejection, or the desire to hold the smooth, hard lines again?

Fuck.

I let my head drop back onto the pillow and stared up at the ceiling. What even *was* the stone? Besides dangerous as hell, that was. And where, in the name of Mary Magdalene herself, had it come from?

The answer had to lie with the woman who'd thrown it to me, but had she even survived? Doubtful, given her condition when she arrived on the shelter porch. But wait —I frowned, making my eyebrows hurt again as I teased details out of the threads of my memories. She'd called my name, I remembered, as if she'd known me … but how? Surely I would have recognized her, if she'd passed through the shelter before. Her voice or her eyes, if not her face. I'd never forgotten any of the women who had stayed there, not even the ones from twenty years ago, when I'd first opened it. I squeezed my eyes shut.

"This is yours now. Find the others," the woman's voice echoed, and my body tensed as it remembered its surge

upward from the ground, its leap for the stone, its collision with my attacker.

Sweat bathed my skin as remembered pain meshed with current. Dear sweet Mary, what I wouldn't give for a painkiller right now—not to mention a sip of water. My mouth had gone so dry that my tongue felt like it had cleaved to my palate, and the drummers in my skull had doubled. At least.

I glared balefully at the call button clipped to the bed near my pillow within easy reach—unless you couldn't move. I tugged at the restraints holding my hands at my sides, but they had a few inches of play in them at most. The button might as well not have existed at all.

From out in the hall came the rhythmic clack of wheels passing by. I wrested my tongue free from the roof of my mouth and called, "Hello?"

The word came out as more of a croak than a call, and the wheel sounds faded away, and the door to my room stayed closed, and no one came to my rescue, and it was just me and—

My gaze drifted back to the pile of clothing. Me and *that* … and the memories of what I had done to the man on the lawn. Not that I regretted defending myself, but *that* had been so much more. It had been … dark. Awful. Unnatural.

I froze as something brushed against my wrists, encircled them, and wound itself around my hands, my fingers. I craned my neck to look down at the left, then the right. I could see nothing, but it felt like—

I inhaled a sharp breath. Cobwebs. It felt like fucking cobwebs, like the ones that had grown from the stone and encased my hand at the shelter, then traveled to cocoon the man and—

I wiped my hands against the blanket, but I couldn't rid

myself of the sensation. My panic ramped up. Ignoring the waves of pain I caused, I jerked against the restraints and yelled for help, again and again until my wrists were raw and my voice hoarse.

And still the spiderwebs remained, invisible but there. Connecting us. Me and the stone. *Not good*, I thought, as I drifted into a fitful, exhausted sleep.

Not good at all.

CHAPTER 6

THE STONE AND I WERE LOCKED IN A BATTLE OF WILLS.

There was no other way to put it. Yes, I knew it was an inanimate object—or at least, it was supposed to be inanimate—and yes, I knew that it had no actual voice, but somehow, on some level, I could still hear it calling me. Just like I could feel its webs threaded around my—no. No, that was just my imagination. All of it. The spiderwebs, the siren call I didn't hear but felt. It had to be my imagination, because none of that could be real.

Concussion, I told myself. *Your brain got scrambled and—*

"Code blue, obstetrics room 521," crackled the intercom in the corridor outside my closed door. *"Code blue, obstetrics room 521."*

I cringed from the memory of another code, called because of me in the emergency ward the day before. It seemed all that much worse now, in the cold light of day. Breaking that poor nurse's nose, running half naked into the corridor, threatening the security guards with the rock.

None of those had been me. None had been things I would do under normal circumstances. Or abnormal ones, for that matter. Concussion was the only answer. It had to be. Heaven knew I had the headache to back it up.

"Code blue, obstetrics room 521."

I forced my thoughts away from the clothes and the stone hidden in their depths and focused on the emergency taking place elsewhere. Obstetrics. That wasn't good. A mother? A child just born into the world? I wrapped my arms around myself. At least they'd taken the restraints off when they'd brought breakfast earlier.

The stone's presence tugged again. I tried to summon words of prayer for the stranger in need to take my mind off it. And off my headache. And off the invisible strands of spiderweb I could still feel clinging to me.

Hail Mary Magdalene, my memory whispered.

"This is yours now," the woman said. *"Find the others."*

"Oh, for fuck's sake," I snarled, just in time for the door to open for a pantsuit-clad figure.

The woman wearing said pantsuit paused mid-step, blinked, stepped backward again to check the room number on the wall beside the door against something on the notebook in her hand, and then looked at me. Well-maintained eyebrows drew together on a forehead stretched tight by severely confined hair.

"Monica Barrett?" she asked. "*Sister* Monica Barrett?"

"Former," I said, by way of explanation for my language—although, to be fair, the decline in my vocabulary (as Mother Annunciata had termed it) had begun long before I formally left the church, and I didn't give two figs what a random stranger thought of it. "I still use the title."

One manicured brow shot upward. "I didn't know you could do that."

"I didn't ask permission."

Brown eyes narrowed as the woman assessed me, or—perhaps more accurately—reassessed, given that I obviously wasn't what she'd expected from a nun. Not even a former one. I sized her up through my headache in turn. Fifty-ish, I guessed. Black, average height and build, and judging from the unusually relaxed fit of the gray blazer that she wore unbuttoned over a pale blue shirt, she carried a—

"Dawson," she said, stepping inside and closing the door. "Detective Sergeant Talia Dawson, Major Crimes.

I've been assigned to your assault case. Are you up to answering some questions?"

She carried a sidearm in a shoulder holster, I finished my thought, because she was a cop.

I opened my mouth to tell her that the police would have been more useful *before* I was attacked, but then I remembered my own assault on the nurse and reconsidered. Charges against me were unlikely, but if the good sergeant had heard about the incident, it might be in my best interests not to antagonize her.

Besides, maybe she had some acetaminophen or ibuprofen on her, because the nurse I'd asked about it at breakfast still hadn't returned—which, given the ER incident, wasn't that surprising. I was still counting my blessings that they'd taken my restraints off.

Before I could ask Detective Dawson about her drug supply, however, the door opened behind her, and a familiar, tiny reed of a woman bulldozed into the room with a force entirely out of keeping with her size. Sister Ernestine, the head of the Sisters of St. Mary's, promptly took up a hands-on-bony-hips position at the foot of my bed and puffed up like an angry hen, every inch of her bristling with righteous indignation. I cringed on the unsuspecting detective's behalf. Whatever Dawson had done to rile the head of the Sisters of St. Mary, she was about to regret it in a major way. Swiftly, I tried to intervene and deflect the Wrath of Erna.

"Sister Ernestine," I began, but I might as well have shouted into the void.

Giving no indication she'd heard me, Sister Ernestine drew herself up to her full five feet two inches and squared off against the cop she'd pushed past.

"Detective Dawson," she said, biting off each word with a snap of her well-maintained teeth. Her originals, she was prone to telling everyone with great satisfaction, whether or not they'd asked. "Did I not make myself clear? I *said* that *we* would let *you* know when Sister Monica was ready to talk."

Detective Dawson stood her ground. "I heard you, but I need her statement while the events are still fresh in her mind."

As if they could ever be anything but. *"This is yours now. Find the others."*

Somehow, Sister Ernestine managed to look over her half-moon glasses and down her nose—both at the same time—at the police detective towering over her. "Do you not have the others' statements already?" she inquired.

"Well, yes, but—"

"Six of them, correct?"

"Well, yes, but—"

Sister Ernestine's chin tilted up another fraction. "Then hers can wait."

The detective craned her neck to look past Sister Ernestine at me, but the nun crossed her arms, stood on tiptoe, and leaned in the same direction to block her view. Dawson heaved a weary sigh.

"I have six statements," she countered, "that make no sense and give me almost no information whatsoever."

She thumbed back a few pages in her notebook, summarizing, "A half-dead woman and her attacker show up on the shelter doorstep, Ms. Barrett takes the woman inside, he picks a fight with the sister, and by the time the uniforms get there, both man and woman have disappeared without a trace. No one knows why they were there, no one saw where they went, and no one can tell me anything more, other than she was dressed in rags and he was—quote, *maybe Russian mob and dressed all in black.*"

I blinked. The woman had disappeared? A wave of

horror washed over me. Dear sweet Mary, had she exploded, too? Oh, how I wished I could speak to Therese and Phoenix and the others.

Dawson flipped the notebook closed. "It really would be helpful if Ms. Barrett—"

"Her name," said Sister Ernestine, "is Sister Monica. And the answer is still—"

The door burst open behind the detective again, and as if summoned by my thoughts, an entire horde tumbled into the room, jostling her this way and that as they—all the women from the shelter—tried to claim a space at my bedside. And to speak at once.

"Sister! You're okay!"

"I can't believe you're alive, never mind awake."

"Oh my god, you look awful! Are you all right?"

"Your poor face!"

"What did the doctors say?"

"I told you he had a crowbar."

I tried to pick out individual voices from the jumble of words, but they all ran together—except for Lissa's remark about the crowbar—and the thud behind my temples grew exponentially worse. I closed my eyes against it, but as soon as I did, the stone arced through my memory toward me, and the hand that had caught it twisted into the blanket. Gritting my teeth, I pressed the fingers of my other hand to the lump at the back of my head. Gently, because sweet Mary, it was one hell of a lump. And I had another on my right temple. And on—

The sound of three sharp claps rang through the room, shocking the women into silence but ricocheting inside my brain. Ouch. I cracked one eye open enough to find a breathless, sweaty Alice standing beside Detective Sergeant Dawson and pointing toward the corridor.

"Out," she ordered the others. "Everyone except Sister Ernestine."

The women grumbled, and Lissa muttered something along the lines of wanting to know who had died and made Alice queen, but a look from Sister Ernestine had her scurrying from the room on the heels of the others. For an instant, blessed quiet reigned except for the normal hospital noises outside—and those damnable drums in my skull—and then Detective Dawson cleared her throat.

"About your state—" she began.

Ernestine and Alice both rounded on her with a resounding, "*No.*"

"It's okay," I said, even though it really wasn't. The headache and I would much rather that Dawson just went away again, but maybe answering her questions would distract me from the stone. "I'll talk to her."

Alice scowled at me over her shoulder. "You were beaten with a crowbar, Sister, and then you—" She stopped short, pressing her lips together so tightly that they disappeared into a single, tight line. Shooting a look at Dawson, she finished, "You could have died. At least wait until we have your X-rays and CT scan back. Your head—"

"My head aches," I agreed, "and I'm a bit sore, but apart from that, I'm fine."

I felt my eyebrows twitch as I realized the truth of my words—and their impossibility after the severity of my attack. I didn't have time to ponder them, however, because Alice wasn't buying it at all.

"*Crowbar,*" she reiterated, her scowl deepening. "So no, you are not fi—"

The door opened again, cutting her off, and a white-coated woman strode in, her attention on the clipboard in her hand. "Good news, Sister," she said. "All your tests came back norm—" Her sentence died unfinished as she looked up from the board and around the room. "Oh. You have company. I'm sorry, I didn't realize."

I waved away her apology and started to welcome her to the party, but Sister Ernestine forestalled me.

"Normal?" she demanded, switching her stare over her half-moon glasses from Detective Dawson to the doctor. "That's not possible. She was hit with a crowbar. Multiple times. And she's sixty-nine years old. No sixty-nine-year-old woman is fine after that kind of attack."

I wanted to agree with her, because heaven knew I *shouldn't* be fine after what had happened—and in some ways, I was far from it—but I knew the doctor was right. Because apart from the headache and some bruises? I flexed my fingers, then rolled the shoulder that had taken the full force of the crowbar. It was unmistakably stiff, but just as unmistakably not shattered the way I thought it had been. The question for me was, how was that possible?

I shifted in the bed, trying to sit up, but Ernestine planted a hand in the middle of my chest to hold me down and pointed with her other hand at the chart the doctor held.

"You're missing something," she said tartly. "Check again."

The young woman in the white coat spread her arms wide, chart in one hand. "We did," she said. "Several times, actually, because you're right. She shouldn't be fine after an attack like that." Her somewhat baffled gaze dropped to meet mine. "You're *sure* it was a crowbar he hit you with?"

"For the last time, it was a goddamn crowbar, all right?" Alice growled. "We all saw it. And we heard it." She stretched out a hand and wiggled her fingers at the chart. "Let me see that."

The doctor—R. Sharma, according to the badge clipped to her lapel—looked her up and down and raised an eyebrow. "And you are …?"

"Alice Jenkins. I'm the nurse at the shelter, and I was first on the scene," Alice replied brazenly, wiggling her fingers again.

Sister Ernestine glanced down at me and gave a tiny shrug. While Alice wasn't telling the full truth, it wasn't an untruth, either. Not altogether, anyway. Dr. Sharma raised an eyebrow at me in a wordless request for permission, and I nodded. With a sigh, she handed the chart to Alice.

The former nurse flipped through it slowly, her eyes traveling one page, then the next, as she shook her head and muttered under her breath. At last, she let the top page settle back into place and handed the clipboard back to Dr. Sharma. She looked down at me, then at Sister Ernestine, then at me again.

"She's right," she said. "It's impossible, but your X-rays and CT scan are all clear. There isn't so much as a hairline fracture in either your skull or your shoulder. You're fine."

Dr. Sharma's mouth drew tight, but she refrained from comment. "You can take over-the-counter pain meds for any discomfort," she told me. "You know the signs of concussion?"

Without waiting for me to answer, she tucked the clipboard into the crook of her arm, pinned it against her chest, and ticked off a list of symptoms on her fingers. "Slurred speech, weakness, numbness, decreased coordination, vomiting or nausea, convulsions, unusual behavior such as confusion, restlessness, or agitation, and of course, loss of consciousness. And if you *were* hit with a crowbar—"

"She was," growled Alice.

Dr. Sharma flicked her an annoyed glance but continued, "—and knocked unconscious—"

"She was."

This time, the doctor clenched her jaw briefly before finishing, "—then I'd prefer to err on the side of caution and have you see neurology next week for a follow-up." She tugged a pen and pad from her pocket and jotted something on the latter before tearing off the page and holding it out to Sister Ernestine. "You'll make sure she goes?"

Alice snatched the paper from the doctor's fingers. "She'll go."

"And someone will stay with her tonight?"

"Several of us," Sister Ernestine assured her.

"Then I'll have someone bring you something for your headache, and you can go home," said Dr. Sharma.

"*After*," growled Detective Sergeant Dawson, "I get your statement."

Sister Ernestine crossed her arms, sniffed her disapproval, and peered over her glasses again. "You have ten minutes," she informed the detective. "We'll wait outside."

CHAPTER 7

 mostly because Dawson kept interrupting to ask questions as if she were conducting an interrogation instead.

"I'm just trying to understand, Ms—" She broke off as I scowled and corrected herself before I could—again.

"*Sister*," she said with an edge to her voice that quite clearly said she didn't understand that any more than the rest of what I'd told her. Or approve of it.

I didn't care. My continued use of the title was none of her business, and I'd told her as much when I'd corrected her the first time. Things had gone downhill from there.

My scowl deepened, and my voice took on a snap of its own. The painkillers the nurse had brought had taken the edge off the headache, but not more than that, and all I wanted right now was to go home.

"And I've told you everything I know," I said. "For the last time, I'd never seen either the woman or her assailant before"—at least, I didn't think I had—"and I don't know what happened to either of them. The woman collapsed on our front porch, we took her in and called the para-medics, the man arrived, and I went back outside to try and hold him off until the police got there. He attacked me and knocked me unconscious, and I woke up in the emergency ward. Whether you understand or not, Sergeant, that's all I have."

It was the Coles Notes version, to be sure, but it was surface accurate, nonetheless. Until I had the chance to talk to the others and corroborate my memories of cobwebs and fire and an exploding man, I had no intention of sharing the additional details.

Scratch that, I had no intention of sharing them, period. Certainly not until I knew what that stone was.

"Why not just lock the door?" Dawson clicked her pen open and shut with an annoying *click-click, click-click.*

I gathered my few remaining shreds of patience and took a deep breath. "Crowbar," I reminded her through gritted teeth. "He had a crowbar, and it would have taken him thirty seconds to smash a window—or the door itself, for that matter—and get inside. *You*"—I pointed at her, meaning the police in general, but liking the sound of the more accusatory *you*—"were going to take ten minutes to get there. At least. The women who live at the shelter are vulnerable, Detective Dawson. It's my job to protect them."

"You. At your age. Didn't you think that was a rather ambitious idea?"

"Two black belts in martial arts," I reminded her. Also for the third time.

Dawson scowled. "Sixty-nine years old," she reminded me in return. Then she waved her pen in an annoyed, *whatever* gesture and heaved a sigh. "Fine. But you must know *something*. As it stands right now, I don't even know what I'm supposed to be investigating here, apart from the attack on you."

I sighed back. "Frankly, neither do I." I shrugged, immediately regretted it when my shoulder twinged, and then pushed away the conundrum of *that* until I'd finished with Dawson. Because I still couldn't quite get past the idea that an ache and some bruises were all I had to show for—

"Do you at least know *why* she came to you?"

A faint heartbeat, not my own, pulsed in the fingers of

my right hand, and I curled them into my palm as my gaze flicked to the pile of clothing on the chair. Once again, the memories surfaced. Images of my attacker turning to run. Of the writhing beneath the lawn. Of the cobwebs engulfing him and the flames rolling away from me to set him alight and then—

I squeezed my eyes shut against the explosion burned into the backs of them. Into me. An explosion that had enveloped an entire man. Or rather, that had *been* him. I flinched from the residual horror, and for a moment, I wavered.

Whatever the stone was, it was big, figuratively speaking, and it was awful, literally speaking. Did I really want to try and figure it out on my own? Maybe I should tell Dawson about it after all. She would want to know. She *should* know. I was always drilling it into the women at the shelter that cooperating with the police was the right thing to do, and Dawson's resources were far more extensive than any at my disposal. Cooperating with her might be my best chance of finding out who the *others* were that the injured woman had said I should find.

Except …

"Sister Monica?" the detective nudged.

Except dear sweet Mary, if the stone *had* exploded my attacker, I had no intention of letting it fall into other hands; and if it hadn't, and I'd imagined the whole bizarre scenario … well. Suffice it to say that I wasn't going to tell Dawson a thing. Not just yet. Not until I knew for certain.

And then it would depend.

Dawson cleared her throat. I cracked open one eye, sighed, and met her gaze with as much lack of guile as I could muster under the circumstances as I finally answered her question with an outright lie.

"I have no idea why she came to us," I told her. "Perhaps she'd heard about the shelter. We're well known in the neighborhood."

Dawson looked pointedly at the pile of clothing, then back at me.

"That's it," she said. Her voice was as flat as her gaze, turning her words to statements rather than questions. "That's your story. You have nothing more to add."

I lifted my chin, silently daring her to call a nun—even a former one—a liar, or to search my clothing without permission. At last she rolled her eyes, clicked her pen closed a final time, and tucked both instrument and notebook into her blazer pocket. From the same pocket, she pulled a business card and dropped it onto the bed beside my feet.

"Fine," she said. "If you change your mind, or any of your residents remember anything, that's my number."

I tried to insist on checking on my charges at the shelter before going back to the sister house, but Sister Ernestine and Alice shot down the idea before I'd even given it full voice. And while I might have won the argument against one or the other, together, the women were a formidable force, especially when my reserves were bordering on empty after the trauma of the last two days. Also especially because I could hardly tell them *why* I was so desperate to talk to the others.

"No," said Sister Ernestine simply, cutting across my, *"I'd like to just check—"*

"Forget it," Alice said when I tried again with, *"But I—"*

I clenched my right hand into a fist to keep it out of my jeans pocket and away from the stone. I opened my mouth to try again, but this time didn't get so much as a sound out before Sister Ernestine tutted and unlocked the passenger door of an ancient station wagon.

"They'll be fine," she said, holding up the sagging door with one hand while she gestured at me with the other. The vehicle, affectionately named St. Jude in honor of the patron saint of lost causes, was held together through the goodwill of our neighborhood garage and a great deal of prayer. It was large and smelly and belched a great cloud of blue smoke when it started, but it ran, and it came in handy for grocery shopping and for taking Sister Julianna —diagnosed a year before with Alzheimer's—to her various appointments.

And, apparently, for unexpected hospital pickups.

Sister Ernestine pushed me into the vehicle and leaned across to clip my seatbelt into place, batting my hands— and my protests—away when I tried to help.

"Sister Carol is at the Mary Magdalene now, and she and Sister Helen and I are perfectly capable of handling things for a day or two," she continued, referring to the woman who was the sixth of our sisters. "You need rest."

Without waiting for an answer, she slammed the door shut and trotted around the front of the car as she headed for the driver's seat. I sighed and rolled down the window —with a crank, because yes, St. Jude was that old—to talk to Alice, who held up both hands to ward off my continued objections.

"Sister Ernestine is right," she said. "You need rest after—" She broke off and flicked a glance across the car roof. "Well. After what happened. And besides, Therese will keep us in line."

The driver's door opened, and I heard Sister Ernestine's keys hit the pavement with a metallic clatter as they slipped from her grasp. She swore under her breath—her language was at least as salty as my own, and she made no apology for it—and I used her distraction to drop my voice, injecting urgency into it as I put a hand on Alice's forearm.

"But that's just it, don't you see? I don't know what happened. I need to talk to the others, ask what they saw—what did *you* see?"

"You don't remember? You don't ..." Alice's voice trailed off.

"Believe what I saw?" I muttered. "How can I? Do you? Do any of you?"

Sister Ernestine's keys rattled again as she retrieved them, then the car sagged as she slid into the driver's seat —testimony to the worn-out shock absorbers rather than her diminutive stature. The car coughed to life, spewed its customary blue cloud, and settled into a sputtering rumble. Alice tugged free of my hand and stepped back, waving away the plumes carried toward her by the breeze.

"Rest," she said. "Talk can wait."

There was something inherently wrong in the statement, but damned if I could put my finger on it. My head throbbed despite the painkiller the nurse had given me; the stone—still hidden in my pocket—felt like it burned against my hip; and Sergeant Dawson's question nagged at me. *"Do you at least know why she came to you?"*

Alice cleared her throat and repeated, "Rest. Please, Sister."

Her voice was gruff, and the concern underlying it was reflected on her face, and it suddenly dawned on me that I'd forgotten a whole other side to the attack—the one where the vulnerable, already-traumatized shelter women had seen me beaten almost to death on the lawn of the place that was supposed to be safe for them. Seen my own vulnerability. My inevitable mortality.

I blinked back the heat behind my eyes as I swallowed —hard. I met Alice's gaze with all the compassion and understanding I could muster.

"I will," I told her. "I promise. And you'll tell the others that I'm okay?"

Her eyes shone with relief and unshed tears. "I will."

CHAPTER 8

As worried as I was about the Mary Magdalene residents, I couldn't deny the relief I felt as Sister Ernestine pulled out of the parking space and I subsided into the passenger seat. Now that the issue of my vulnerability—and mortality—had belatedly dawned on me, the aftermath of my ordeal was settling into my bones with a vengeance. Holy Mother, if I hurt this much today, I was going to be really sore tomorrow. And the day after. And probably the one after that, too.

But at least I had survived, I reminded myself. And by some miracle, I was mostly unharmed, and that was something. Unbidden, my focus zeroed in on the hard lump sitting against my right hip bone, and my mouth compressed.

That was something, too.

"Are you sure you're okay?" Sister Ernestine asked. We sat at the parking lot exit, waiting for a break in traffic, and she twisted in her seat to study me with narrow-eyed concern. "I can take you back inside and make them keep you another night, if you'd rather stay here."

I had no doubt she could make good on the promise—or threat, depending on how you wanted to look at it—but I rejected the offer with a tiny, careful shake of my head. "I'm fine. Really. But I suspect you and Alice were right about sending me home to bed."

That and a shower, because sweet Mary, I needed one of those—and a change of clothes. I wasn't sure what felt crustier at the moment: my sweat-stained shirt, my grass-stained jeans, or my sweat and grass-stained skin. The hospital had offered a shower, but Sister Ernestine hadn't thought to bring a change of clothes, and there hadn't seemed much point in me being clean if my clothes weren't as well.

"Twenty minutes," Ernestine promised, turning her attention back to the busy street and tightening her grip on the steering wheel. "I'll have you home in twenty minutes."

St. Jude inched forward, and I let my head drop back against the seat's headrest. The stone's presence in my pocket tugged at me again, whispering for my attention, but I resolutely ignored it. Whatever it was that the woman had tossed to me, whatever it had done to that man, whatever it wanted from me—it would have to wait, at least until I was alone, because no way on Earth would I chance exposing someone else to …

Well, whatever it was.

Closing my eyes, I focused on the familiar rumble of the car's engine, the bumpity-bump of failing shocks over rough streets, and the hot, city-scented breeze coming in through the window. For all of our neighborhood mechanic's skill, the air conditioning was not something she'd been able to keep going.

In the last fading seconds before exhaustion claimed me, the inherent wrongness of not returning to the shelter prickled at me again, but even as I tried to surface into it, it slid away.

And then, so did I.

SISTER ERNESTINE SHOOK ME AWAKE IN THE DRIVEWAY OF the brown brick house that was home to me, her, and four other nuns. I blinked in the late afternoon sunlight streaming through a gap in the giant maple tree overshadowing the front yard. Along the width of the house ran a sagging porch, currently occupied by two women clutching one another's arms and anxiously watching the vehicle. I smiled. It was good to be home.

And then I jolted upright.

I had it. I knew what was wrong with me being here. More specifically, with me being *not there*. Not at the shelter.

I whirled in my seat to face Ernestine, seizing her wrinkled hand in my own. "What if someone else comes?" I demanded. "What if he didn't act alone?"

Ernestine frowned. "Comes where? Who?"

"The shelter!" I tried to dial back the impatience in my voice and slow my words—and my racing thoughts. "What if someone else comes to the shelter looking for—" *Shit.* Ernestine didn't know about the stone. Unless … maybe Alice had told her? Unless Alice hadn't seen it herself. Maybe none of the others had. Maybe—

The world wobbled before my eyes, and momentary panic—make that greater panic—gripped me.

Sister Ernestine turned her hand over in mine and gripped my fingers. "Breathe," she said.

"I am," I wheezed with the last of the air in my lungs, because no, no I was not breathing. I gritted my teeth and inhaled through my nostrils, deep into my belly, focusing on the in, then the out. Then I did it again. The world righted itself, and the panic receded. The certainty I was right, however, did not.

"The shelter—"

"They're taking precautions," Ernestine said. "I've told them what to watch for, and they'll take turns at both the front and the back. You"—she gave my fingers an extra squeeze—"need to worry about yourself for the moment.

You may be the strongest and fittest among us, but you're still sixty-nine years old, and you took one hell of a beating."

At least, that was what I thought she said, because I hadn't processed much after *"I've told them what to watch for."*

I blinked at her. "What to watch—but how—what—"

Sister Ernestine released my hand and patted my cheek. "Later," she promised. "After you've eaten and slept. And after we've made sure that"—she jabbed a finger in the direction of my lap, as if she knew what I carried in my jeans pocket—"is somewhere safe. At least for now."

Now I blinked *and* flapped my mouth at her. "But— wait—how do you—"

She shook her head and placed her index finger over her lips in warning as she nodded past my shoulder at the house. "Hush," she said. "The others are coming, and they're not all part of this. For their own safety, they mustn't be, Monica. Do you understand?"

Part of what? Understand what? I wanted to ask—sweet Mary, I had so *many* questions all of a sudden—but Ernestine was already taking the key from St. Jude's ignition and climbing out of the driver's seat, and the passenger door beside me was opening and the concern and compassion of our fellow sisters was enveloping me and—

Without warning, my brush with mortality slammed into me with the force of a wrecking ball—or a crowbar— as I realized just how lucky I was to be home. To be here. To be *alive.* I'd been in my fair share of street fights over the years—okay, maybe more than my fair share, given my calling and age—but never had I come that close to—

Gentle hands reached across me to unclip my seatbelt, and then one slid behind my bruised shoulder and a second cupped my elbow, and I looked up into the soft, worried brown eyes of Sister Ruth.

"Come into the house," she urged. "Let's get you comfortable."

I hesitated for an instant, my mind going again to the shelter and the women there, to the trauma they'd endured and my responsibility to keep them safe from more, but Sister Ernestine stood behind Ruth now, and the determined set of her shoulders and jaw held an unspoken reassurance. I might not know what was going on, but I was willing to believe that she did. And to let that be enough for now.

Because holy Mother, that really had been a close call. Too close.

Far, far too close.

Trembling beneath the weight of fatigue and my newfound, unfamiliar, and unsettling fragility, I let my companions tug me from the car and steer me toward the house.

Chapter 9

Once we were in the house, fatigue and self-perceived fragility rapidly gave way to a feeling of overwhelm when I found myself subjected to more fussing than I'd ever known.

Or ever wanted.

I had been the caregiver all my life, ever since my mother had died when I was twelve, and my father had considered it my responsibility to raise my six siblings, including the newborn infant he'd refused to have anything to do with. The baby had been born intersex, an abomination in Father's eyes, and he'd told us that God had taken Mom as punishment. He'd never spoke of it or her again, and I had become de facto mother, a role I'd never stepped away from, even after I left home to enter St. Paul's Monastery.

So, finding myself at the mercy of four women intent on looking after me now was new, uncomfortable, and … intense. I wanted a shower, pajamas, and bed. Instead, I found myself digging deep in search of appreciation, and deeper still to hide my irritation as a variety of sweaters and blankets, pillows and cushions, plates of sandwiches, and cups of tea were brought forth.

The moment the door closed behind us, Sister Julianna guided me to her coveted recliner and pushed me into it, then dived to raise the footrest with so much enthusiasm that both chair and I almost toppled over backward.

Then, as soon as Sister Helen righted me, Sister Ruth pressed tea into my hand, with a good dollop of brandy added to it for fortification, she said, and Sister Ernestine whisked it away again because of the pain killers I'd been given, and …

And with every fiber of my being, I longed for the peace and privacy of my own room—not to mention the time and brain space I needed to come to terms with what had happened at the shelter. Or, at least, what I *thought* had happened.

Because the more time that slipped between me and the memories, the more impossible the latter seemed. If the others hadn't been there—Phoenix, Lissa, Danelle, Alice, Tonya, Rebecca, Cindy and Therese—if they hadn't seen the woman, too, hadn't seen the attacker, hadn't seen him—

I put the brakes on my racing thoughts, because they *had* been there, of course. And Alice's words at the hospital assured me they'd seen what I'd seen. Some of it, anyway.

I inhaled a short, sharp breath, and instantly, Ruth and Julianna were at my side. Ruth took the cup from me and set it on the side table, and Julianna took the plate of uneaten tuna sandwiches, retreating with it to a corner of the room. Then, putting the back of her hand against my forehead, Ruth *tsked* with concern. That did it. I could take no more.

I shoved the recliner's lever forward to drop the footrest, then pushed myself out of it. Pain enveloped me from my throbbing head to the soles of my feet. Grimly, I swallowed it. Any display of weakness would only invite more attention, and I had officially run out of depths that I could plumb in search of appreciation. Or patience.

"Enough," I said—or maybe growled, given how still the room went. I gritted my teeth and tried to soften my abruptness by adding, "Please."

Nope. Even I wanted to wince at the snarl in my voice. I sighed.

"I'm sorry," I said. "I appreciate the concern, really I do, but I'm not hungry, and I'm not thirsty, and … " I trailed off. The next part was unavoidable, but an aching fatigue tugged at my entire body, making me hesitate. I needed to know what was going on, but I needed sleep, too, and—

"And?" Sister Ruth prompted.

I squared my shoulders. As much as every atom of me longed for bed—hell, I could even forgo the shower right now—I knew that I wouldn't sleep. Not yet. Not when the stone sat heavy in my pocket and the shelter on my conscience.

"And Sister Ernestine and I need to talk," I said, meeting the other's gaze across the room. "Now."

We left Sister Helen cleaning up the tea things and Ruth trying to relieve Julianna of the tuna sandwiches before she spoiled her dinner. I followed Sister Ernestine down to her office, a windowless cave of a room in a low-ceilinged and otherwise unused basement that the others believed was haunted in some way.

The room, Sister Ruth had confided to me when I was helping with dishes one night, had been here when the Sisters of St. Mary had moved into the house, but it had been very different then. Its floor, walls, and ceiling had all been painted red, she'd said, and then she'd looked over first one shoulder and then the other before dropping her voice to a hushed whisper and adding, *"And there was a dead-bolt on the outside of the door."*

She and Carol and Julianna were convinced that something awful had taken place there—torture was Ruth's guess—and they'd wanted to permanently barricade the room. Sister Ernestine had told them they were being dramatic, however, and had claimed it as her office, removed the deadbolt, slapped four coats of a deep, forest-green paint over the red, and installed a vinyl plank floor. All, Ruth had confided, shaking her head in a gesture that seemed more awed than disapproving, while burning an inordinate amount of sage and muttering incantations that were not quite … in keeping with the church.

If my admiration for the tiny but formidable head of the sister house hadn't already been cemented at my suitability interview with her, it certainly would have been with Sister Ruth's story. Sister Ernestine, to quote Phoenix at the Mary Magdalene shelter, rocked.

And so did her office.

Sister Ernestine had added a hodge-podge of furnishings and lamps to the room, none of which matched—and none, I hazarded, that were less than fifty years old—but the overall effect worked. Lined with overflowing bookcases, the space was cozy, inviting, and—given that the others, with the occasional exception of Sister Helen, refused to set foot in it even after thirty years—private.

In short, it was perfect for the questions I needed to ask. And the answers I hoped Sister Ernestine could give me.

Descending the stairs to the basement had, however, highlighted all the bits of me that hurt at the moment, and a part of me seriously regretted not postponing this conversation until morning. That part crossed the room, lowered herself gingerly into a plump armchair, and swallowed a whimper when her bruised bones settled into the softness.

The other part of me, the one that couldn't get the stone off her mind or shake her concern about the women at the Mary Magdalene, fixed Sister Ernestine with a forthright glare.

"What the fuck," it said, "is going on?"

Sister Ernestine held my gaze for another few seconds,

then crossed the room to stand beside me. She held out her hand, palm up.

"May I see it?" she asked.

I stiffened. "What—how—"

"Therese told me the woman threw something to you. Show me." She waggled her fingers.

I considered denying that I had anything, but what was the point? Lying to my friend to hide something that I never wanted in the first place? And still didn't want? I eased my aching rib cage to the left and lifted my hips far enough off the chair that I could slide my fingers into my jeans pocket and retrieve the stone. I held it out on the flat of my palm.

It sat black and unmoving—as a stone should—about two inches square and roughly a half-inch thick, its surface polished. I half-hoped Sister Ernestine would take it from me—then wondered what I would do if she tried, because my fingers twitched with an urge to close at the very thought that she might.

But the nun didn't touch it. Instead, she switched on a lamp sitting on the desk, grasped my wrist, and tugged my hand into the pool of light. She leaned down to study the stone. Then she exhaled a long, slow breath.

"So, the stories were real," she muttered. She shook her head, stared at the stone for another moment, then her somber gaze met mine. "I'm sorry."

I blinked, her apology momentarily distracting me from the *stories being real* idea. "For what?"

"That." She nodded at my hand. "I suppose I always thought it was a myth, that they could do that, but ..." She trailed off, shaking her head, and repeated, "I am so, *so* sorry, Monica."

Wait ... *they*? Did that mean this thing wasn't the only one out there? My gaze followed hers back to the stone in my palm. And what did she mean, she'd thought it was a myth? A myth that they would do what, exactly?

Then I saw, and my breath caught on a sharp inhale. They were back. The spiderwebs were back. I hadn't imagined them in the hospital after all. Under the pool of light from the desk lamp, there was no mistaking their presence. No mistaking their realness. And they were woven not just across the surface of the stone, but through it. And not just around my hand, but through that, too. And Sister Ernestine could see them.

A tiny bubble of pure, unadulterated horror formed in my chest, just behind my breastbone, because holy Mother of All, how was that even possible? How was any of it possible? The stone, the spiderwebs, the exploding man … the *spiderwebs*.

I tore my gaze from the strands winding through and around me, joining me to the polished, square rock, and glowered at a resigned, sad-looking Sister Ernestine.

"*What* fucking myth?" I snarled.

And then the lights went out.

Chapter 10

The power came back on within seconds, thanks to the standby generator installed by a church benefactor some decades ago, after an ice storm—one of the benefits to remaining on the institution's good side. But by the time it did, Sister Ernestine was already across the office and wrenching open the door. I gaped at her with a befuddlement born of sleep deprivation, pain, and shock that the murder-stone had somehow become attached to me. Then, as she disappeared out the door, reaction kicked in.

I bailed out of the chair and stuffed the stone back into my pocket, wondering briefly at being able to do so if it really was attached to my hand. Then I abandoned the question and hurried in Ernestine's wake.

And what a wake it was. Sister Ernestine had always moved with purpose, but I'd never seen her move this fast. She made a beeline through the dim basement, and even at fifteen years her junior, I was hard pressed to catch up.

"What's going on, Sister Ernestine?" I huffed at the foot of the stairs, and again as she reached the top and burst through the door into the kitchen. "Sister Ernestine! What's going on?"

Without answering, she pushed past a startled Sister Helen, who stood with ladle in hand by the stove, and raced down the hall toward the front door. I shrugged at Helen's raised eyebrows, brushed past her as well, and set off in renewed pursuit of the other nun. I found her standing on tiptoe, peering through one of the little windows at the top of the door.

"Fuck," she muttered under her breath. "Fuck, fuck, *fuck*."

"Sister Ernes—" I began.

She dropped back down to her heels. "It's only our house," she said.

"What is?"

"The power," she snapped.

"How can you tell? It's still light outside. Maybe—"

"The neighbor's porch light is still on across the street."

The across-the-street neighbor's porch light was always on, I started to point out, but then I stopped, because perhaps that was the point she was trying to make.

"Maybe it just came back on already," I suggested. The heavy thrum of the generator at the side of the house contradicted me, however, because it wouldn't still be running if that were the case. I frowned at the thought, wondering through my headache—and the befuddlement that seemed to be my new norm—why it should be a problem.

"Don't you see?" Sister Ernestine grabbed my shoulders and gave me a shake, and a shaft of pain went through my shoulder. "No one else lost power. Only us. That means they've found you."

She didn't wait for my response. She shunted me to one side, released her hold on me, and barreled back toward the kitchen, bellowing for Helen. I stared after her, and then her words sank in. *"They've found you."*

Pain, discomfort, and befuddlement all evaporated in a rush of adrenaline. I leapt for the door, dropping the security bolt into place and fumbling for the deadbolt. I could see that it was already locked, but I needed to be sure. Needed to put every possible barrier between me and what might be coming.

What I knew *was* coming.

Because I might not know who *they* were, but I sure as hell knew what could happen if they got into the house and I had to face them again. At the side of the house, the rumble of the standby generator died into silence. I flicked the switch beside the door for the hall light above me. It didn't come on. I turned and ran for the kitchen.

Sister Ernestine was in the middle of barking orders when I got there.

"—and call Sister Carol," she said, pointing at Sister Helen. "Tell her to get all the women inside the shelter and lock the doors and windows. She's not to open them for anyone."

Sister Helen didn't so much as hesitate. The ladle she'd been using dropped into a pot of spaghetti sauce, splashing red across the stove and countertop. Ignoring the mess, she pulled a cell phone from the pocket of her flowered pinafore-style apron with one hand and switched off the no-longer-functioning element beneath the simmering pot with her other. Sister Ernestine continued past her into the dining room, her pace not slowing.

I followed yet again, reaching the doorway between the living and dining rooms as the nun swept the knickknacks from the fireplace mantel and stretched up to press on a brick—the third from the top on the left-hand side.

The front panel of the oak mantel dropped open. My jaw did likewise.

Except my jaw didn't have a hidden compartment behind it—or a small armory within.

The blood drained from my face. I knew because I could feel it pooling in my toes, and there was a sudden buzzing in my ears and a feathery feeling in my skull, as if my head had filled with cotton candy.

"The fuck …?" I croaked.

But Sister Ernestine wasn't done. She lifted the top of

the mantel and locked it open, displaying an array of weapons, and her nose wrinkled as she considered the options. Then she pulled a lethal-looking shotgun—

Hell, who was I kidding? *All* the guns in that cubbyhole were lethal.

I made another attempt to pull myself together and pointed at the shotgun that was almost as long as Ernestine was tall.

"Sister Ernestine, what the hell is going on?"

Her gaze flicked over me, then settled beyond my shoulder. "Sister Carol?" she asked.

Behind me, Sister Helen's worried voice responded, "No answer."

"Damn it." Ernestine stuck her hand back in the cubby, this time pulling out a box of shells. "All right. Call the police and—"

"They'll take forever to get there. They always do," said Sister Helen.

"Call," Ernestine repeated.

Helen nodded, but as she took her phone from the apron pocket again, a pounding at the front door made us all freeze. Sister Ernestine was the first to move, spinning around to stare at me over her glasses.

"Is that them?" she demanded.

"What?" I gaped back at her, almost as dumbfounded by the question as I was by the sight of a shotgun-toting Sister Ernestine and a secret armory. Almost.

"Is. That. Them?" The nun bit off the words, the volume of her voice increasing with each one.

"I don't—how—" I gave my head a shake to try and clear it, because none of this made sense. Them *who*? And how in the name of Mary Magdalene herself could I possibly—

More hammering, this time at the back door. Sister

Helen dived toward the armory and grabbed a handgun, and Ernestine whirled to face Ruth, steely determination in every line of her face, her body, the way she hefted the shotgun.

"Take Julianna down to my office," she said, "and lock the door."

"But we can help," Ruth said, starting toward the fireplace. "I remember how—"

Sister Helen intercepted her. "No, Sister Ruth," she said, her tone gentler than I suspected Ernestine's would have been—and entirely at odds with the fact that she was shoving a magazine into the base of the pistol she held. "We know *you* remember, but Julianna ..."

She let her voice trail off as we all looked toward the eldest and frailest of us, who paced back and forth between television and sofa, muttering under her breath and flapping her hands in agitation. Stress almost always triggered a dementia episode for Julianna, and—

Well. Suffice to say that I was pretty sure the commotion on the porch, the hammering on the back door, and the discovery of hidden guns in the house counted as stressful. They certainly did for me.

Sister Ruth hesitated for a second, then nodded. She crossed the room to Julianna's side as a crash out on the front porch made the house shudder. Sister Julianna jumped and tried to swat her away, but adept at soothing her colleague, Ruth ducked past her flailing arms and leaned in to whisper in her ear.

I couldn't hear what she said, but Julianna's arms stilled, and her taut, frantic expression relaxed into a tentative smile. Sister Ruth took her hand and led her toward the kitchen and the basement stairs there. Much like the obedient child to which she reverted now and again, Sister Julianna followed without argument. She stopped beside me and looked back at Ernestine and the shotgun, and then turned her gaze to mine.

"Be safe," she said, and then added wistfully, "I'll miss you."

The front door crashed open.

CHAPTER 11

"Honey, we're he-ere," a deep male voice boomed, cutting across Julianna's shrieks and Ruth's frantic attempts to soothe her as she steered the terrified woman toward the kitchen and the basement stairs.

I'd already put myself between the nuns and whoever was about to come into the living room before I'd even registered moving. My headache had slowly been ramping up again, and now, with no painkillers remaining in my system and my blood pressure skyrocketing, its throbbing had become relentless, vicious. The pain in my shoulder wasn't far behind. But apparently, my instincts still worked just fine. There was a small amount of comfort in knowing that.

Less comfort in knowing that this would be my second fight in as many days, that I was feeling every single one of my sixty-nine years, and that I still had no idea what the first one had been about. Or with. Who *were* these people coming after a bunch of elderly nuns—and what in the name of Mary Magdalene herself was this stone that they wanted so badly?

The loading of a round into a shotgun chamber snapped me back to the immediate. I shot a look over my shoulder at Sister Helen beside me with pistol in hand, and Sister Ernestine on her other side with the shotgun butt to her shoulder and the barrel aimed at the doorway.

Heavy footsteps approached, slow and methodical as our intruder strode down the hallway toward the living room. I tipped my head to one side to listen. No, not intruder. Intruders, plural. At least three.

My every fiber sagged at the thought. I'd barely survived one yesterday. If they had weapons and Ernestine and Helen went down …

I flicked a glance at the array of guns still in the mini armory. I'd never fired—or held—a gun in my life, but attempting it now might be safer than expecting my body to endure another physical confrontation. But even as I hesitated, the footsteps stopped outside the living room door, and Sister Ernestine stepped between me and the open mantel.

"Run," she said, pressing a set of keys and a plastic bank card into my hand. "Take the car and get as far away from here as you can, and then *keep* running. I wish I had time to explain, but what you have—the stone—they can never get it, do you understand? You have to keep it away from them, no matter what."

Fear and anger snarled together inside me, and I tried to push the card and keys back at her. "I don't understand, no. They who? And what in Mary's name *is* the damned—"

The question died on my lips as the living room door swung open, and my gaze flashed to the opening. Three figures stood there, two of them flanking the obvious leader. They were all dressed—as my earlier attacker had been—in black. Black jeans, black turtlenecks, and black leather gloves.

None, however, carried a crowbar, or any kind of weapon that I could see, and a tiny hope flickered in my chest, because three of them, three of us, and we had guns on our side. Maybe—?

"Oh, look," said the man at the front of the little group. "You were expecting us. And here I'd hoped we'd surprise you."

"Leave," Sister Ernestine snarled in return. "Leave now, and no one gets hurt."

The man, pale skinned and looking as if he hadn't seen the sun in months, if not years, smiled as he stripped the gloves from his hands. He handed them to one of his companions, then lifted his right hand and held it out before him. I caught my breath. Was that—

It was. It was fire. Sweet Mary, he had flames dancing in his palm, flickering in shades of deep purple and crimson. Fire. And he was lifting his other hand and shaping the flames into a ball, and it was growing, and—

The deafening retort of gunfire—many shots grouped together— slammed against my ears. The doorframe near the man's head exploded into splinters of wood, and the figure to his left staggered backward and toppled to the floor. The remaining two dived out of sight to the sides of the doorway, and I looked around to find Sister Helen with her weapon trained on the fallen man as Sister Ernestine pumped a fresh cartridge into her shotgun chamber.

Slow shock enveloped me as every part of my being recoiled from what my brain told me had just happened. Helen ... Sister Helen, who had never so much as squashed a spider, who'd driven an hour out of town to release a groundhog she'd caught in a live trap in her vegetable garden ... Sister Helen had just *shot* someone? And Sister Ernestine had, too, and—

Purple and crimson fire flared in my peripheral vision. Instinctively, I threw myself to the side, into the scant shelter of Julianna's recliner as the fireplace—and the small armory it contained—exploded in a shower of brick fragments and twisted metal.

Gunfire sounded again, and I clapped my hands, one still clamped around the bank card and keys, over my ears. Peering around the chair, I expected the worst—or the best, depending on how you wanted to look at it—but the doorway remained empty, and there were no additional bodies in the hallway beyond it. Just the one. Which meant the others had dodged and were—

I inhaled as the hallway glowed a sinister, red-streaked purple. Whatever the intruders had thrown at us, there was more coming, and this time, they might not miss. If the exploded fireplace was any indication, neither my companions' guns nor my black belt skills would stand a chance against it. Which left—

A hard hand seized my arm as my fingers inched toward my jeans pocket and the stone within. Sister Ernestine glared down at me, her brown eyes fierce above the half-moon glasses.

"No," she said. "You need to go, Monica. We'll buy you as much time as we can, but you need to go *now*."

I hesitated, torn between loyalty and the urgency in her voice. Behind her words. My gaze slid sideways, toward the malevolent glow in the hallway. If the stone did again what it had done yesterday afternoon, I had no doubt that it would give me the upper hand—or at least a fighting chance—but for how long? How many more would come after whatever it was?

"They can never get it, do you understand? You have to keep it away from them."

Sister Ernestine's hand lifted my chin, and I met the determination in her gaze. The determination, the calm, the resignation ... and once again, the sadness that underscored them all.

"Run," she said again.

I clutched the card and keys tight in my fist, staggered to my feet, and bolted from the room.

No one intercepted me on my flight through the kitchen, out the back door, or around the house to the driveway. But it took three fumbling tries to get the key inserted into St. Jude's ignition, and four desperate twists of that key before the car grudgingly rumbled to life. With my foot on the brake, I slammed the gear shift into reverse—

And then I sat there, staring at the house I was about to leave. The one I knew without doubt that I would not be coming back to if I *did* leave. Indecision gripped me. The purple and crimson flames had been so bright—surely someone had seen them, or at least heard the gunshots. Not all of the neighbors worked. Some of them had to be home, and if they were, and they'd called 911, help might already be on the way, and if it was—

"Run," Ernestine whispered in my memory. *"Keep running."*

Fuck.

I slammed both my hands against the hard plastic of the steering wheel, once, twice—

My hands froze in mid-air as a blinding flash of light from the house seared my vision, followed by a rumble that shook the leaves of the maple tree overhanging the yard and made St. Jude lurch to the side. I watched in horror as the house began a slow crumble into splinters and bricks and dust and then erupted into flames, taking with it the only home in which I'd ever really felt *at* home—and the sisters who had made it that way. The women I had loved like family—but not just any family. Like *sisters*.

Shouts reached my ears through the car windows as neighbors poured from the surrounding houses and arrived from the bordering streets. Some of them started toward the shattered, burning house, and instinctively, I reached for the door handle, wanting to go with them. Needing to see whether someone had survived. Desperate to try and—

I froze as a stumbling figure emerged from the smoke

and flames. My heart leapt for an instant, then it stalled, then it turned to ice and plummeted. The figure was distinctly male. Tall, broad-shouldered, and about the same size and shape as the man who had stood in the living room doorway and summoned the crimson and—

I ducked low behind St. Jude's steering wheel as, dust-streaked and black-clad, the figure stopped in the middle of the lawn beneath the maple tree's spreading branches and turned to survey the damage—and to look around as if searching for someone. It was definitely him.

And he'd see me the second I pulled out of the drive-way. Fuck. Panic sucked the air from my lungs and—for a frantic few heartbeats—wiped the ability to function from my brain. Then, bless the blind goodness of their hearts, a group of elderly neighbor ladies descended like a flock of birds around the man, one of them placing a blanket around his shoulders despite the sweat-inducing heat, another pressing a glass of water into his hand.

"Run," whispered Ernestine again.

A last second of hesitation gripped me, tangling with my grief and threatening to hold me captive as her words pulled me one way and my love for her and the others another. With a superhuman effort, I shook it off. Tears spilling from my eyes and running down my cheeks, I gulped in a shuddering breath and settled my hands around the steering wheel. I had to move. Now, while whoever was under that blanket was still distracted.

With a long, last look at the house and the flames that shot outward in every direction from it, I backed out of the driveway and onto the street. There, heart shattered, I headed west, blinded both by my tears and the sun that rode low in the early evening sky. I had no idea what I was running from, or where I was running to, or what it was that I carried with me, but I was damned if Ernestine and Helen and Ruth and Julianna had died for noth—

I slammed on the brakes, barely even registering the shriek of tires behind me as the car behind me did likewise.

Ernestine and Helen and Ruth and Julianna … but not Sister Carol. Because Sister Carol was at the shelter, and she hadn't answered when Helen had tried to call, and—

The shelter.

A car horn honked, and I looked into the rearview mirror. The blurry reflection of a man in a vehicle behind me waved impatient hands, but the part of me that might have otherwise cared was absent, and all I did was stare. He leaned on the horn a second time, then yanked on his steering wheel and pulled around me, tires squealing when he floored the gas pedal, again when he slammed on the brakes long enough to give me the finger, and a third time when he peeled away and fishtailed down the street, narrowly missing the fire truck speeding toward us.

I returned my gaze to the rearview mirror and the fire truck pulling up in front of the remains of the house I'd left. A second one joined it from the other direction, and firefighters spilled from both onto the street and lawn. I wiped my wet cheeks with the back of my hand.

The Sisters of St. Mary would be found now. Found and turned over to the church and cared for in a way that I no longer could, because I needed to leave. To run, as Sister Ernestine had said. And I would. But not yet. I couldn't, because running from the sister house—leaving them behind the way I'd done—had used up every internal reserve I'd possessed and some I didn't know I'd had. I didn't have the strength to abandon the shelter, too.

Not without knowing.

Chapter 12

The shelter was gone.

I sat in St. Jude, half a block away and stared at the police barriers and uniformed officers holding back the gawkers who had come to take cellphone pictures and videos. At the police car straddling the intersection ahead of me, blocking vehicle traffic. At the yellow *Do Not Cross* tape bobbing gently in the breeze, stretched across what had once been the front yard of the Mary Magdalene House for Women.

The shelter that was just …

Gone.

The sun's setting rays streamed across the city onto the charred, smoldering ruins that remained, turning plumes of smoke to orange and yellow. Firefighters came and went, gathering equipment and rewinding hoses as they walked across the picket fence that had been knocked down and trampled into a lawn now more mud than grass. Their trucks—three of them—lined the street in front of the yard, along with three police cars, the fire chief's SUV, an unmarked police sedan, and four paramedic vehicles.

An unmarked police sedan meant detectives, I thought numbly, and paramedics who stood somberly by their vehicles in no rush to leave meant—

I gulped for air and clawed back a sob that tried to escape. *How many? How many didn't make it out?* I thought about the women the Mary Magdalene had sheltered, and the bonds that they had forged. They'd all survived so much just getting here. Worked so hard to rebuild themselves. Deserved so much more from life. Losing any of them was unthinkable. Losing all of them was too immense for words.

"Run," whispered Sister Ernestine's voice in my head, and my hands spasmed on the steering wheel as sudden fury bubbled up from my belly and turned to bile in my throat. I choked it back.

"Run *where?*" I demanded of her memory. "Where the *fuck* am I supposed to go, Ernestine? What am I protecting? And who the hell—"

A tap on the window beside my head cut off my stream of questions. I twisted in my seat, instinctively reaching at the same time to unclip my seat belt. Part of me was ready to vault across the console and bolt from the vehicle—and a greater, angrier part of me readied for battle.

Both parts recoiled in shock as I recognized Phoenix's tear-stained face on the other side of the glass.

For a moment, I could only stare at her, dumbfounded. Then she visibly sniffled, swiped her sleeved forearm under her nose, and motioned for me to roll down the window. I nodded furiously, fumbling for the crank. It promptly fell off in my hand, and I tossed it into the back seat and thrust open the door instead.

The instant I stood on the sidewalk beside her, Phoenix fell into my arms, shaking and sobbing and utterly incoherent. I gathered her as close as I could and held her tight and let her cry, uncaring that my own tears soaked the top of the head buried against my chest. Uncaring that St. Jude still rumbled and hiccupped at my back. Uncaring that a handful of people had turned to stare at—

A frisson of caution whispered over my skin. No. The staring, I needed to care about. The staring, and the people, and—my gaze flicked over the watchers and then beyond. No one stood out as having anything more than mild curiosity, but still …

I shifted my hands to Phoenix's shoulders and held her away from me. "The others?" I asked the question because I had to, not because I expected a positive response.

Her bottom lip quivered, emphasized by the ring piercing it. She shook her head. "Sister Carol—" Her voice broke and she gave a little hiccup, then tried again. "Sister Carol sent me to get milk, and when I—when I came back—"

She stared past my shoulder and her eyes filled with fresh tears. "Oh God," she moaned, wrapping her arms around herself and sagging toward the ground. "All of them ..."

Gritting my teeth against the strain on my shoulder, I held her upright. I wanted nothing more than to fold up with her, to sink to the pavement and wail my anguish, but the frisson of caution across my skin had become a prickle of instinct. I still didn't think anyone was watching with more than passing interest, but I couldn't take the chance. Not of being seen, and not of being captured on video and put up on social media somewhere.

We couldn't take the chance, because I had Phoenix to think about now, too.

"We have to go," I told her. She kept staring past me, and I gave her a little shake to get her attention. "Phoenix. We have to go."

Watery blue eyes blinked up at me. "Where?" she asked. "Your house with Sister Ernestine and the others? I don't think she likes me much."

Renewed anguish filled my throat and tried to steal my voice. I shook my head. I happened to think that Phoenix was wrong about Sister Ernestine, but she didn't need to know that. Not right now. Not anymore.

"No," I whispered. "We can't go there."

Phoenix's eyes went wide, processing what I'd said ... and what I hadn't. "Them, too?" she choked.

"Them, too."

She looked past me again. "Then where?"

"I—" I cast about in my mind for an answer, but I had none. "I don't know," I admitted, "but we can't stay here."

Phoenix considered my answer for a few seconds, then swiped her arm under her nose again and nodded. "Okay," she agreed. "What about the milk?"

She pointed at the ground by her feet, and the cotton grocery bag sitting there—cotton, I remembered, because hard-as-nails Lissa had vetoed plastic, insisting we do our part for the environment. I swallowed the lump in my throat—a lump that was made up of the memory of her, of the memories of all of them.

So very, very many memories.

I pushed them all away. I would have time to remember later, I hoped, but for now, I had the stone and Phoenix to protect. And a whole lot of *what the fuckery* to figure out before the next attack came, because I was absolutely certain there would *be* a next attack.

"Leave the milk," I told my charge gruffly. "Let's just go."

CHAPTER 13

RUNNING WAS ONE THING. RUNNING WITHOUT A PLAN OF some kind—any kind—was quite another. Especially when the car you were driving went through gas the way the women at the Mary Magdalene went through Tonya's prized chocolate truffle cake when we were able to afford the ingredients.

My breath snagged at the thought, and I determinedly filed that memory away with the others behind the imaginary door I'd constructed in my mind to hold them back. To keep them from spilling out and clouding what was already the murkiest of situations.

I sent St. Jude's fuel gage a baleful look. The tank had been full when we left the scene at the shelter because Ernestine liked to keep it topped up—another snagged breath, another memory added to the others—but we were down by almost half already, and we were still driving aimlessly around the city, crisscrossing the core again and again. North to south, east to west, rinse and repeat.

It had been a plan of sorts, I supposed. Kind of. Get to where there was the most traffic, where there were the most people, where we had the best chance of hiding in the weekend crowds. But it had still been daylight then, and it wasn't now. The sidewalks were all but empty, and traffic had thinned to the point where we were sometimes the only vehicle sitting at a traffic light.

We were definitely going to need a new plan.

I signaled for a left-hand turn and glanced sideways at Phoenix, who had curled into the smallest possible ball against the door and fallen asleep. She looked lost in the expanse that was St. Jude's passenger seat. Lost, and fragile, and—I gritted my teeth. And what in Mary's name was I going to do with her?

My stomach grumbled as I waited for the oncoming traffic to clear, reminding me that I hadn't eaten since breakfast. Between Dawson and doctors and visitors, my lunch tray had sat untouched, and I hadn't had so much as a bite of the tuna sandwiches Ruth and—

My appetite evaporated in yet another rush of memories, but Phoenix—I looked across the car again—Phoenix definitely needed to eat. Plus, I could do with a break from driving in circles. Whether the thought of food appealed or not, I suspected I would think more clearly with at least a muffin under my belt. Even if I had to choke it down.

I turned my attention to our surroundings, trying to get my bearings. I'd been letting buildings and streets flow past in a blur as I drove, not paying attention to much other than not getting into an accident, but the signs with Chinese lettering lining both sides of this street made my task easy. We were in the heart of Chinatown, where restaurants abounded. Even better, many were of the small, dimly lit variety, where I would be able to see someone coming through the doors before they could see me.

Half a block ahead, a car pulled out from the curb, and I aimed for the parking spot it had vacated. With a great deal of back-and-forth maneuvering—and a great deal of muttering under my breath—I coaxed St. Jude into the space between a Mercedes sedan and a BMW convertible, then switched off the engine. The engine hiccupped into silence, and I leaned across the seat to touch Phoenix's arm.

"Phoe—"

The young woman jolted upright before her name was

halfway out of my mouth, startling the crap out of me. I pulled back with a smothered squawk of surprise, triggering a second reaction from her, and another from me, and another from her, and—

We stopped and stared at one another in the light spilling into the front seat from the streetlight outside. My lips twitched, and then hers. Then she giggled and I chortled, and then we both bellowed with laughter …

And then we didn't.

Hers changed first. A laugh that caught halfway through on a great, heaving sob as she flung herself across the console and into my arms. Once again, I caught hold of her thin body and held on tight, as much for my own sake as for hers. Briefly, I considered trying to hold back my own tears, but they were so many, so fierce, and so awful that I thought they might drown me from the inside. So I let them go, and my own sobs mingled with Phoenix's until I couldn't tell one voice from the other. Until it didn't matter.

We cried for the shelter and the family we had lost there. For Alice and Lissa and Danelle, for Tonya and Rebecca, and Therese and Cindy and Sarah. We cried for the Sisters of St. Mary—for Ernestine and Carol and Helen and Ruth and Julianna. And then we cried for us.

At least, I did. I cried because I was sixty-nine years old, and I hurt all over, and I'd been certain I was going to die yesterday, and now I was here and all the others were gone, and I had no idea what had happened or why, or what it was that I protected, or what I was supposed to—

Gentle fingers brushed my cheeks, wiping away my tears and jolting me back to the front seat of St. Jude and to Phoenix. With an effort made a thousand times greater by the thumping in my skull, I sniffled my way into silence and opened puffy eyes to find Phoenix watching me in concern.

"Oh God, Sister," she said. "I forgot all about what happened to you yesterday. You must be in so much pain—not to mention exhausted. We should find somewhere to eat, and then we can talk."

She nodded in agreement with herself, then leaned back and dug fingers into the pocket of her tattered jeans. "I still have the bank card Sister Carol gave me for the—" She broke off, her expression stricken, then tightened her jaw and handed the card to me. "For the milk," she finished. "We can use that."

I took the card from her, letting my fingers close around hers. "Thank you," I said. "Food is an excellent idea." And not just a muffin, either.

Then, because I was supposed to be the one looking after her instead of the other way around, I pulled her in for a quick hug. "I'll find somewhere for us to go, I promise," I told her fiercely. "I'll keep us safe, and I'll figure out who that woman was yesterday, and I'll find out what the hell is going on."

Phoenix turned her head against my shoulder and stared out the windshield for so long that I decided she didn't believe me—probably because I didn't believe myself—but her gaze when she drew back and lifted it to mine was determined rather than doubtful.

"About that," she said. "I have an idea."

CHAPTER 14

"An internet café?" I frowned at Phoenix over the piece of broccoli I'd fished out of my pho bowl with my chopsticks. "Do those even exist anymore?"

The young woman in the red vinyl booth across from me rolled her eyes. "Not everyone has the money to buy their own computer, you know."

Of course I knew that, but because I considered computers to be more of a nuisance in my life than the blessing everyone else seemed to consider them, I had to admit to not having given it much thought. Phoenix had been in charge of keeping the rather aged machine running at the shelter, and for teaching the other residents the computer skills they needed to get jobs—legitimate ones. However, apart from having an email account, I had clung to my paperwork ways.

"Fair point," I said, biting into the broccoli floret and speaking around it. "So what will we do there?"

"You'll probably just watch," replied the shelter's—the former shelter's—techie dryly. "But I might be able to find out where the woman came from."

In a heartbeat, my brain went from a sense of relief at Phoenix's apparent recovery from the trauma she'd endured to an utter standstill. For a moment, I froze altogether. I stopped chewing, stopped blinking, stopped breathing. Hell, I wouldn't have been surprised if my heart had stopped beating.

But no, it pumped valiantly on, and the rush of the blood that it pushed pounded in my ears. I swallowed the broccoli and laid my chopsticks across the bowl of soup.

"You know who she was." It was a statement rather than a question, but Phoenix nodded anyway.

"She told us her name before she went out on the porch," she said.

"Alice—" My voice wobbled on the name, and I curled my hands into fists under the table and tried again. "Alice didn't tell me."

"She said you needed to recover first."

Momentary irritation flashed through me, and then I slumped back against the bench seat and nodded, because in all fairness, I would have done the same in Alice's shoes. But why hadn't she told Detective Dawson? Loyalty to me? Something else? Had the mystery woman told her more than she'd told the others? I blinked back a prickle behind my eyes, knowing I would never have the answer, and cleared my throat.

"And?" I prompted.

"Sister Margaret."

Shock rippled down my spine, making me straighten up again. A nun. The woman had been another nun. Had Sister Ernestine known? Had Alice told her, and was that why she'd told them to take precautions at the shelter? What had she been about to tell me when the power went out at the sister house? What in the name of Mary Mag—

Another, more immediate question interrupted the babble flowing through my mind. "No last name?" I asked Phoenix.

She shook her head. "Not that I could understand, no. She was pretty far gone and already running out the door when she told us, and then afterward, she was just ... gone. But I maybe if I see it, I'll recognize it. That happens sometimes, right? When something triggers your memory?"

I sighed and tried not to let the complete dashing of

my hopes show on my face. "It does," I allowed, "but Margaret is a common name among nuns, especially ones her age. I've known at least three myself ..."

I trailed off, remembering how the woman on the porch had known my name. Was it possible that she had been one of the Margarets I had known? But from where? There had been the one who'd stayed with us at the sister house last year, and the lawyer I'd met through my work with the shelter, and—

"Was there anything else that you noticed about her?" I asked Phoenix. "Was she wearing a cross? Some orders have particular styles that they wear."

Phoenix again shook her head. "No cross," she said. "And no tattoos like you, either. At least, not that we could see under all that dirt."

"She wouldn't have had a tattoo, no. Not if she was still part of an order." I glanced down at the NO REGRETS etched on my hand. Yesterday, the words had shored up my resolve. Today, they made me question the many other choices I might have made that would have changed events. Choices such as waiting inside the house for the police like Detective Sergeant Dawson had suggested. Or telling her about the stone. Or insisting that Sister Ernestine take me back to the shelter after I was released from hospital.

Or staying with Sister Ernestine and the others and using the stone again. Letting its webs wrap around me, through me ...

I shuddered and covered the tattoo with my right hand, grounding myself in its intent. *No regrets* had never been about blithely believing I'd done everything right, I reminded myself. It was a reminder not to dwell on a past that I could not change. A past that now included yesterday and today.

I squared my shoulders and reached again for the

chopsticks. "It's a good idea," I said, fishing a chunk of chicken from the broth, "but without more to go on——"

"That's why we need an internet café ," Phoenix said. "She was in awful shape, Sister. Wherever she'd been, she'd been there for a while, so I was thinking that someone may have reported her missing, which means there might be a report somewhere. If I can find that, we'll know where she came from, right?"

I had to admit that her idea held merit, but could it be that simple?

Phoenix rested her elbows on the table and leaned toward me, sensing my wavering and pressing home her advantage. "At least give me a couple of hours for … research."

I narrowed my eyes. She'd had me until that hesitation. "Research?" I echoed.

Phoenix's earnest gaze slid away from mine and dropped to her pho bowl. She picked up her chopsticks and twirled them one way through the rice noodles, then the other. "I can find her," she said stubbornly.

I raised an eyebrow. "Legally?"

She hesitated. "How about ethically?" she countered. "Ish."

Alarm bells went off in my head, and I was shaking it in the negative before she'd even finished. "No. Absolutely not, Phoenix. Sweet Mary, if you're caught hacking again——"

"I won't be. I'll be fast—and careful. I know how to cover my tracks, and I'm not going after sensitive information. I'll only be looking at the national database for missing persons."

"Aren't those public record? Can't we just call and ask someone?"

"If we call someone, it will take time for them to look it

up. And they'll want to know who we are and why we're asking. And there's a good chance that the detective who came to the house has flagged our names because of the"—Phoenix paused to swallow hard, then continued—"because of the shelter. And if the sister house is gone, too, then you—well. Let's just say my way will attract less attention. And it's faster. Besides, it's like those existent circumstances cops always talk about, right?"

"*Exis*—

I felt a smile tugging at my mouth, but I took care to hide it. "*Exigent* circumstances?" I suggested.

"Yeah, that."

Given that our lives were very likely in real and present danger, I supposed these *were* exigent circumstances, but I rather doubted the police would see it that way. It was on the tip of my tongue to tell Phoenix so, when the restaurant door swung open, and a rowdy group jostled their way in.

They were no threat to us—or to anyone. They were just friends out for a late dinner and harmless fun. But by the time my brain processed that fact, Phoenix had already shrunk down in her seat, eyes wide and face taut, and my hand was halfway into my pocket, my fingertips brushing the stone within as the spiderwebs wrapped around my wrist, and every fiber of my being was primed for fight or flight.

Shaking, I pulled my hand free of my jeans and curled it into a fist on my lap beneath the table. There had been no threat … this time. But what if there had been? The half-bowl of chicken pho I'd consumed had helped, but it wasn't nearly enough to repair the ravages of the past two days. I was still exhausted, and my sudden tensing had made my entire body scream at me, some parts—like my shoulder—louder than others.

I could be as primed as I liked for fight or flight, but the truth was, I didn't think I could fight my way out of a paper bag right now—or that I'd make it as far as the door if I tried to run.

Plus, I had Phoenix to think about.

And I still didn't know where I was going.

Fuck.

I uncurled my fingers and rested them on my thigh. I needed to get a grip and make some decisions. Closing my eyes, I made myself focus on my breathing. Three long, slow breaths … in through my nose and out through my mouth. Slowly, I coaxed my body to relax, starting at my toes and working my way up one muscle group at a time: feet, calves, knees, thighs.

I'd reached my shoulders when someone dropped a dish in the kitchen, shattering it and any pretense that I was going to achieve ease. Not here. Not tonight. And sure as hell not after what had happened to the others and was likely coming after us. I opened my eyes to find Phoenix watching me, still hunched down in her seat, now with the hood of her hoodie pulled up over her head. Her earlier confidence had dissipated, and once again she looked small and fragile and lost.

A pang of sorrow for her sliced through my heart. The losses of today had been bad enough for me, but they were infinitely worse for someone as young and vulnerable as she was.

"Are you okay?" she asked, making a visible effort to rally for me.

I was not, but on the other hand, I had to be, and so I dodged the question.

"Finish eating," I said brusquely, picking up my chopsticks and pointing them at Phoenix's bowl. "Then we'll find what you need."

The term *internet café* turned out to be a bit of a misnomer, in my opinion. The place that Phoenix directed me to was a tiny hole-in-the-wall establishment with blacked-out windows and graffiti-covered bricks on the outside, and nothing that in the least resembled dining tables or food on the inside. Unless you counted old, cheese-flavored nacho chips as food.

I did not.

But the café was open around the clock, the disinterested clerk accepted my bank card as payment for three hours of internet access, and the computer equipment earned a nod of approval from Phoenix as she claimed a station in the back corner near the washrooms—and, I hoped, near a back exit, if we needed one.

Just in case.

My personal tech assistant glanced up at me as she logged on with the code the indifferent attendant had scrawled on a slip of paper. "You may as well get comfortable," she said. "This will take a while."

I looked around the room at the available furnishings. The café was little more than a tunnel lined on both sides with computer stations, twenty in all, and the chairs backed onto one another with just enough room to navigate between them if you needed to go pee—or to run from men out to kill you. A few of the chairs were of the high-end fancy kind that hardcore gamers used, but those were all occupied, and I suspected that said occupants had paid a premium for them. The rest of the chairs ... were not.

It was going to be a long three hours.

I selected the one that looked like it might have the most padding and eased my body into it. Every joint complained, and judging by the especially tender spots, additional bruises had surfaced since the hospital. Getting out of bed tomorrow was going to be a serious challenge.

My thoughts hiccupped as I remembered I no longer had a bed. Or a home. Or—

No. I wouldn't go down that path right now. Not tonight. It was too fresh, and I was too tired, and the earlier tears were threatening a return, and … just no.

"You okay?" Phoenix frowned at me, her fingers continuing to dance across the keyboard.

"I'm fine," I said.

"Liar."

"Are *you* okay?" I countered.

"Not even a little," she responded. Then, as she turned her attention back to the monitor, she added, "We're not supposed to lie, remember? House rule."

I snorted. Smart-ass kid. "Noted," I said. "I'm sorry, and you're right. I'm not okay, but I will be. So will you. And no, that's not a lie."

She echoed my snort but said nothing more, fully immersed now in her task. I watched the lines of code unraveling on the computer screen for a few minutes, but there was nothing I could do to help, and so I arranged my bruises around the chair as best I could and slid down in it until I could lean my head against the back. Within seconds, I slipped beneath the surface of my exhaustion, lulled by the *tappity tappity* of the keyboard keys.

CHAPTER 15

IF PHOENIX'S SHOUT OF WARNING HADN'T WOKEN ME, THE vehicle coming through the internet café's storefront would have done the trick. It plowed through chairs and computers alike, tossing debris and bodies the length of the room before coming to rest in the center.

I surfaced out of sleep amid a screech of metal against concrete and bolted from my chair, throwing myself across Phoenix and carrying her with me to the floor, then shoving her under the table. Clambering to my feet again, I widened my stance and raised my hands into a defense pose as I faced the vehicle and tried to figure out what the hell had just happened.

Dust filled the air, highlighted by the flickering lights that hung by their wires from the ceiling. Someone near the front of the café screamed in pain, someone else cried in deep, guttural sobs. A dark SUV sat at a lopsided angle atop a pile of rubble, its windshield an opaque screen of glass shattered into a thousand pebbles that still clung to one another. The remains of the internet café's door sat atop its hood like a mangled pretzel. A puddle of blood spread outward from beneath the mound of wreckage.

My hands drifted back toward my sides as the extent of the carnage sank in. Holy Mother of—

Metal squealed again as the SUV's passenger door swung open, and my hands came back up again, one before me for protection, the other drawn back and ready to strike. An enormous man climbed out of the seat onto the rubble and picked his way down the front of it to stand, uncaring, in the crimson puddle. All six-foot, five-inches of him. At least.

So. Not the same one as at the sister house. I wasn't sure if that was a good thing—as in we hadn't been followed—or a bad one. As in, how many people were after this stone of mine, anyway?

I shored up my resolve as cold eyes regarded me. I couldn't make out their color in the flickering light, but their expression? That was unmistakable.

"Enough," their owner said. "Give us the stone, and you might live."

I considered denying any knowledge of the stone but dismissed the idea before it had completed itself. The black-dressed hulk of a man facing me wouldn't believe me, and he would have no qualms about breaking me into pieces in order to search for the stone himself. A stone I had no intention of letting him have. Certainly not on purpose.

Which meant there was no way this was going to end without a fight.

The question was, what kind of fight was it going to be? The physical crowbar kind, or the fiery, blow-up-everything one? I wasn't too keen on my chances either way, unless …

Above the screams from the front of the store—underscored now by someone else's shouts for help—I heard the wail of an approaching siren. I hoped it was more than one, and that they were heading here. Because if I was going to stall for time, I'd like it to work. I drew a steadying breath.

"Apart from that sounding like a line from a bad movie," I told the veritable giant of a man, "you should probably know that there's no *us* anymore. There's just you."

He glanced over his leather-clad shoulder—what was it with these guys and their leather in this heat?—to the closed driver's-side door. Swiftly, fruitlessly, I scanned the room for a potential weapon while his attention was otherwise occupied. Verbal stalling would only get me so far. More than likely, I was still going to have to engage.

The giant snorted and turned his attention back to me, a spark of amusement in his eyes now. "And you see that as an advantage for you?" He chuckled. "Have you looked in a mirror lately, grandma?"

Normally, I liked nothing better than being underestimated by a potential opponent based on my appearance. This time, however, my opponent had a point. Even standing several feet away from him, I had to tip my head back to look at him.

Keep stalling, I told myself, *and no, don't look for Phoenix. She'll be fine. She is fine. She has to be.*

"I'm willing to take my chances," I said. With all the nonchalance I could muster, I tilted my head to one side and then the other, then rolled my shoulders to loosen them. An audible crack emanated from the one that had taken the crowbar impact. The giant chuckled again.

"As am I," he said. He extended his hands up and out to his sides and flexed his fingers.

Shit. It's going to be the fire fight.

I thought about the stone in my pocket, but the exploding first attacker on the lawn of the shelter made me shy away from the idea. Keeping the stone from this man —and all the others who seemed to be trying to get hold of it—might be important, but it didn't mean that I could risk using it with so many others in the immediate vicinity. I needed to find another way.

The man facing me had none of my qualms, however,

and his fingers were twitching and dancing at the ends of his hands. Whatever he was doing looked nothing like what the leader at the sister house had done, but I had no doubt that it would be just as bad. I scanned the wrecked room again, this time looking for somewhere I could shelter from whatever was coming at me, but the SUV had taken out every table in the room except the one that I'd thrown Phoenix under.

Phoenix, who had pulled the monitor and keyboard down onto the floor with her and was madly typing away. Was she still—? I tore my gaze away from the young woman and her computer as tiny blue sparks danced at the corner of my vision. Sparks that were coming from the tips of the man's fingers.

I quickly evaluated what I might be able to ask my body to do for me. It wasn't much. I gauged the distance between me and him—too much—then between me and Phoenix—not enough. The sparks danced higher, became brighter, crackled audibly over the chaos in what remained of the front of the internet café. Like it or not, a fight was coming before help got here. I took a deep, steadying breath and sank back into my training. My instincts.

My focus narrowed to just me.

Just the man.

Just the stone in my hand.

I did a double-take. Hell, how had that gotten there? Too many people around, I reminded myself, trying to stuff the stone back into my pocket, but it was too late. The webs had already encircled my wrist like tentacles, and I could feel them meshing with the sinews and veins in my hand, and—

The first bolt of blue lightning came from the man's left hand. Caught off guard, I was too slow to duck and instead threw my stone-bearing hand up to deflect it. White-hot agony raced down my arm to my core, then down my legs and out the soles of my feet. I staggered— but I didn't fall. A second bolt flew toward me.

I dived toward the floor, intending to tuck and roll back up onto my feet in a move that I had practiced hundreds, if not thousands, of times. But the stone had other ideas. The tuck and roll still happened, but instead of me gaining my feet as planned, momentum carried me forward until I lay flat on the floor beside broken cement blocks and a mangled, bloody arm that extended out from beneath them.

A horrified breath whooshed from me. Another, equally horrified one whooshed back in.

It was happening again. My hand was stuck to a floor this time instead of a lawn, but everything else … everything else was the same. Silvery strands stretched outward from my fist and the black stone clenched in it, writhing across the floor and through the puddle of crimson to wind themselves around the man's boots. Just as they had done with the man at the shelter, they climbed his legs and twisted around his torso, reaching for his arms and face and throat.

Just as before, his mouth opened in a scream—but this one wasn't silent.

It was primal. Guttural. Filled with a terror unlike any I'd ever heard.

And then, just as before, the fire started. First in the stone that grew hotter and hotter, then spreading to my hand and through me from head to toe, turning my insides to liquid flame, my bones to molten lava. Panic licked at me, but I quelled it. I'd lived through this the first time, I told myself, and I would do so again.

The panic receded a little, and I reached beneath it to the calm I knew to be at my core. The calm of long practice, of discipline, of experience. Ignoring the fire trying to consume me, I closed my eyes and breathed into it. *Hail Mary Magdalene, full of grace, come and sit with me.*

The stone softened and began pulsing in my grasp like a small, beating heart, and the fire consuming me pushed outward, seeking release. Seeking … prey.

I doubled down on my journey to calm. Inhaled. Exhaled.

Hail Mary Magdalene, full of grace, come and sit with me.

The man's screams abruptly dropped off, and I fought the urge to open my eyes and look to see why. I knew why. I knew the cobwebs had engulfed his face and his voice. I also knew what would come next, and I wanted no part in it. I fought to keep my focus on my center, on the fire and not its intended victim. On not doing again what I had inadvertently done before.

Hail Mary Magdalene, mother to us all, come and pray for me … pray for him … pray for—

"Ma'am! Ma'am, are you all right?" Strong fingers felt for a pulse at my throat, then jerked away. "Jesus! She's burning up—can I get some help back here? Hey! I need help back here!"

The fire in me became liquid flames, boiling over and out and—

No. No, I would not do this.

"Fuck!" I bellowed, and with a strength that wasn't mine, I gritted my teeth, tore my hand from the webs encasing it, and rolled onto my back. For a moment, I could see nothing but the yellows and oranges and reds of the fire that consumed me from the inside out, but then the heat abruptly abated, the flames flickered out of existence, and I was left staring up the police officer kneeling over me.

He stared at me for a long moment as horror warred with astonishment in his expression. Then, without word or warning, his eyes rolled back in his head, and he keeled over onto the floor.

CHAPTER 16

A paper mug of steaming liquid appeared under my nose, and I stared at it a moment before poking my hand out from under the blanket to accept it. Given the steamy September night gripping the city, both blanket and hot beverage seemed counterintuitive, but encroaching shock said otherwise.

I was cold to the very center of my being. Cold and exhausted, and—

Well. Paranoid didn't even begin to describe the level of my hyper-awareness as I scanned the thinning, wee-hours-of-the-morning crowd behind the police barriers on the other side of the street. Had that tall man at the back been there the last time I looked? What about the stocky one on the fringes to the left? Or—

"It's probably more effective if you actually drink it," a dry voice observed above me.

Detective Dawson's dry voice, because of course she'd had my name flagged in their system, and of course they'd called and gotten her out of bed to come here, and--

I looked up to meet her bland gaze, then down at the mug again. "Thank you," I mumbled.

Bending my head, I sipped the tea she'd brought me and almost gagged.

"I added extra sugar," she offered. "The paramedics said it would be good for shock."

Prior warning would have been nice, but I appreciated the gesture. I made myself swallow the overly sweet concoction, wincing when it hit my already-unhappy stom-ach. I didn't remember feeling like this after the previous

… incident, but neither had the previous incident ended quite like this.

I decided that I didn't like either ending.

"Well?" Dawson asked. "Are you going to tell me what the fuck is going on?"

Another decision: I would much rather not.

"The cop that passed out," I asked instead. "Is he okay?"

"He's fine."

"And Phoenix Where is she?"

"Answering some questions," the detective sergeant replied. "Which is what I'd like you to do."

"What is she answering questions about?"

"Trying to hack into the police database. But I'm sure you already knew that."

I was too tired to even attempt a poker face. I sighed and sipped again at the tea syrup. "How much trouble are we in?"

"*She* will likely get off with a warning, given that she didn't actually succeed. You, on the other hand …" Dawson trailed off. She put a sneaker-clad foot beside me on the bumper of the fire truck where I sat. "I know you're a former nun and all, but encouraging someone with her record to break into the national police database? Really?"

"It's … a long story."

"I'm all ears."

"You wouldn't believe me if I—"

The rattle of wheels against concrete interrupted me, and I looked over at the ruined storefront to see two paramedics wheeling a gurney out onto the sidewalk. A body bag was strapped onto it, the fourth of the night.

My stomach rolled again around the tea in it. The accident victims had already been taken away, which had left only one body inside the building after Dawson steered me out: the man who had been swathed—the man *I* had swathed—in a cocoon of spiderwebs. I watched in silence as he was loaded into the back of the last remaining ambulance.

Fuck.

"This is all connected, isn't it?" Dawson pressed. "To the shelter and the Sisters of St. Mary burning down yesterday? And your attack the day before?"

Had all of that really happened in just two days? The very idea seemed surreal, as if my mind couldn't quite connect all the dots anymore. As if there was just too much space between the thoughts. Or perhaps between my brain cells themselves.

I pressed my lips together, wondering what my chances would be if I threw the tea at Dawson and bolted for St. Jude, still parked half a block away under a streetlamp. I sent the beat-up old station wagon a wistful look, feeling its age in my own bones, because truth be told, neither one of us was up to outrunning the cops.

Plus, if Phoenix had failed to hack into the police database and find a missing persons report for Sister Margaret, we still had nowhere to go.

"Monica."

I looked up at Dawson again, wondering if her dropping of my *Sister* title was deliberate.

"You wouldn't believe me," I said again. "Hell, *I* don't believe me."

"Maybe I will, and maybe I won't," she returned equitably, "but I'm really not seeing much choice here."

I thought hard about that for all of three seconds, which was how long it took to acknowledge that she was right, and that I could go no further on my own. With a sigh, I set the over-sugared tea on the bumper between me and the detective's foot and reached into my jeans pocket for the stone.

Dawson regarded it, one eyebrow raised as far as I thought it could go. "It's a rock," she said.

"I wish," I muttered.

Her gaze flashed to mine, and she frowned. "If you're trying to be cute—"

"Do you have a flashlight?" I asked.

"I beg your pardon?"

"A flashlight. Do you have one?"

She pursed her lips and narrowed her eyes, clearly debating whether she should humor me or just arrest me. Then she grumbled under her breath and pulled her cell phone from its holster at her waist. Switching on the flashlight function, she held it between us, pointing it toward my lap. "Will that do?"

Without answering, I moved my hand and the stone into the bright pool of light and motioned for her to lean closer. Another grumble, but she took her foot from the bumper and set it on the ground, then did as I asked.

"What exactly am I supposed to be looking—oh!" Dawson's startled exclamation accompanied a hasty step away. "What the fuck—"

The phone's light flashed into my eyes, and I blocked it with my other hand until she lowered it to the stone again. Gingerly, she returned to her study of the stone and the silver filaments running through it—and me. I blinked away the spots, then, in the glow from the phone light, watched her expression shift from disbelief to fascination to horror and back again. Her gaze lifted, and she scowled.

"Those are—that's—what the fuck—"

"Spiderwebs," I said, filling in the blanks. "Impossible. And I don't know. But a lot of people seem to want it, and they're willing to kill for it, and I can't let that happen."

Dawson reached to take the stone from my palm, and I closed my fist over it.

"I *won't* let that happen," I clarified.

Her scowl deepened to a glower. "You know I can arrest you."

"You can," I said, choosing not to add that any attempt to do so would not go well. "Or you can help me." I leaned back to slide the stone into my pocket again, then adjusted the blanket around my shoulders and clutched it tight. "Look around you, Sergeant Dawson. Look at what they're willing to do—and at what the stone can do. You saw that man. You saw what happened to him?"

She gave a single, terse nod of her head.

"Well, if the police had gotten here ten seconds later, you wouldn't have," I said wearily, "because he would have disappeared, just like my attacker did at the shelter."

"Disappeared?"

"Exploded," I elaborated. "Or burned to ash. Or both, maybe. I didn't see how it finished, but whatever happened to him in the end, he basically evaporated. That's why your people didn't find anything in the way of remains on the shelter lawn."

Dawson's eyes had turned hard, and her jaw clenched and unclenched. As I'd predicted, she didn't want to believe me. But neither could she deny the last thirty-six hours. Both the Mary Magdalene shelter and the sister house had been burned to the ground, one man had disintegrated altogether, an SUV had plowed through the front of an internet café leaving a swath of death and destruction in its wake, and another man had been carted away in a cocoon.

Whether either of us wanted to believe me or not was pretty much moot at this point. As was whether any of this remained a police matter. Or the fact that I was at the center of it all.

Dawson switched off her phone's flashlight and pocketed it. Crossing her arms, she stood back to watch the first responders still moving about the scene. I watched her, in turn, but her face was hard to read now that it was in the shadows.

At last she asked, "Your friend, Phoenix—what was she looking for?"

"The woman who came to the shelter gave them her name before she disappeared." I poked a hand out from the blanket and held it up to ward off the accusation I sensed forming on Dawson's lips. "Before you say anything, I didn't know about it myself until tonight. The shelter— the women—" I gritted my teeth, clutched the blanket harder, and made myself finish, "The shelter residents agreed not to tell me until I'd recovered from the attack."

Calling them that—*the shelter residents*—seemed almost obscene, given what the women of the Mary Magdalene had meant to me and Phoenix. But words, I had found, could sometimes create distance when it was needed. If I wasn't going to fall apart again, this was one of those times.

Dawson grunted noncommittally. "Go on."

"She was a nun. Sister Margaret."

"A nun-nun, or a pretend nun?"

I waited without responding, and the detective sergeant sighed.

"Sorry," she said. "That was uncalled for."

"Apology accepted," I replied, "and I have no idea. She may have given a last name, but Phoenix didn't hear it clearly and doesn't know what it might have been."

"So, hacking the database was to …?"

"Check to see if anyone had reported her missing.

Phoenix—*I,*" I corrected, because given Phoenix's juvenile record, it was far better that I take the blame, "thought it would be faster to check the national system than to start making random calls."

"Which would raise questions," she said astutely.

"Yes."

Another grunt. "It's not the worst idea I've heard," she said. Then, "What makes you think she might have been reported missing?"

"Her condition."

"The way she was dressed, you mean?"

The residents really hadn't told her much, had they? Although neither had I, when I'd given her my statement in the hospital. I answered her question with a shake of my head, shuddering as I recalled in excruciating detail the emaciated woman on the porch. Her matted hair, her paper-thin skin, her stench ... the fragility of her very bones when I'd carried her into the house.

"It was more than that," I said. "She was skin and bone—skeletal, really. And absolutely filthy. If I had to guess, someone had been holding her captive for days, if not weeks. And starving her."

"Hell. Seriously? And no one thought to tell me any of this?" Dawson threw her hands wide and paced in a circle. "We could have already had an ID for her. Found out where she was from. Started looking for whoever ..." She trailed off as the ambulance with the cocooned man in it drove past us.

It used neither lights nor siren, and we watched in silence until the taillights disappeared around a corner. Then Dawson's gaze returned to mine, and her mouth twisted into a tight, unhappy line.

"Exactly," I agreed.

More pacing, this time with hands on hips in silence. I

waited, scanning again the few stragglers who remained along the barricade. The tall man at the back and the stocky one at the edge were both gone. Coincidence?

Time would tell.

"You know I could lose my job over this," Dawson said finally.

"I know."

"Fuck," she muttered. "Everything about this is wrong, but—fine. I'll run some checks and see what I can find. Where are you staying?"

It was my turn to snort, and a hint of pity flashed across her face.

"Sorry," she said. "I forgot you're …"

"Homeless?" I supplied tightly.

"I can call around to the shelters—the other shelters, I mean. See if they have room."

"I don't think I want to take that chance, thanks. If we're found again …" I sent a speaking look at the shattered storefront. "Besides, we have St. Jude. That will do for tonight."

She cocked an eyebrow. "St. Jude?"

I pointed down the street. "The station wagon. It's a bit on the cranky side, so Sister Ernestine named it—" I swallowed the snag in my throat and tried again. "Sister Ernestine named it after …"

"The patron saint of lost causes," Dawson finished gruffly. She studied the sagging boat of a vehicle. "You sure that's a good idea, staying in it? You'll be a sitting duck."

"Shelter," I reminded her. "House. This." I waved my hand. "Seems to me St. Jude is as safe as anywhere, right now."

"Touché." She cleared her throat. "Right. Do you have a cell phone?"

"No."

"Money?"

"Some." I had no idea how much was in either of the accounts, but I made a note to stop by an ATM later and find out.

"Good. Get a burner," she said. "Something prepaid. Text me the number when you have it."

"Where?"

"Pretty much any corner store will have them."

A corner store would have an ATM where I could take out some cash and check bank balances, too, so that would be two birds, one stone. That worked.

"You still have my business card?" Dawson asked, reaching into her pocket.

"Same clothes as the hospital," I replied, pointing a finger at my grass-stained jeans, now caked with concrete dust as well. "So, yes."

She withdrew her hand again. "Good. I'll check missing persons in the morning and let you know as soon as I have anything. *If* I have anything."

"Thank you. And Phoenix? What about her?"

Detective Sergeant Dawson made a sour face, as if I was asking one favor too many, then rolled her eyes. "She'll be out in a minute," she said. "But no more internet cafés. I'm holding you a hundred percent responsible for her, understand?"

"Oh, believe me," I said quietly, "I'm well aware of my responsibility."

The detective had taken a dozen steps down the street when she stopped and turned to me again. "Why former?" she asked.

"Pardon?"

"You told me at the hospital that you're a former nun," she said. "Why former?"

Hail Mary Magdalene, full of grace, come and sit with me …

"Many reasons, Detective," I replied. "Many, many reasons."

Hail Mary Magdalene.

DAWSON WAS AS GOOD AS HER WORD. TWO MINUTES AFTER the detective left me on the bumper of the fire truck, a uniformed cop brought Phoenix to join me. The relief on the young woman's face when she saw me sent a stab of remorse straight to my core. I stood, letting the blanket fall to the ground, and she wrapped her arms around me in a fierce hug.

"I'm *so* glad to see you!" she said.

The knife blade of remorse twisted sharply. "I'm so sorry," I told her. "I should never have agreed to this. Letting you hack into—what was I even thinking?"

She drew back. "You think *that's* what I was worried about?"

Well, yes, because it was certainly what *I'd* been worried about. That, and her being arrested and potentially going to prison, because *police database.* I didn't have a chance to say so, however, because Phoenix was already waving a dismissive hand and then hugging me again.

"I was worried about *you*, Sister. That man—the cobwebs—that blue lightning—and then the fire. It was just like the first time, on the lawn. You turned so bright that I thought you'd caught fire again—that you were dead."

I closed my eyes as she squeezed harder. So. The fire thing wasn't just my imagination. Awesome.

"You have *got* to stop scaring me like that," Phoenix continued. "You're—"

She broke off, and holding her away, I pursed my lips and lifted a brow.

"I'm what? Too old for this?" I inquired, knowing full well that was what she'd stopped herself from saying. It was what everyone had been saying today—yesterday—whatever—and I was getting damned tired of it. Not to mention damned tired, period.

Phoenix didn't answer—or meet my gaze—and general crankiness drove me to continue, "I'll have you know that I'm in better shape than most people half my age, young woman, and I'm—"

"All I have left," she whispered, cutting my self-righteousness off at its knees. "You're all I have left, Sister. I can't lose you, too."

Oof. I rocked back on my heels and closed my eyes as my indignation drained from me. I'd been moving so fast ever since I'd picked her up from the sidewalk outside the shelter—running, thinking, trying to come up with a plan—that I hadn't stopped to think about the full impact all of this might have had on her. She and I shared grief, yes, but for her, there was so much more.

She had lost the only place that had welcomed her as she was. The found family that had loved her back. The bedroom that had been hers and hers alone, unshared with foster siblings or unwanted companions or anyone she didn't want there.

She hadn't just lost the shelter and the family in it; she'd lost her stability. Her security. Her safety.

Under the circumstances, I really was all that she had left.

Which, under those same circumstances, was *not* a good thing. But neither was it a topic either of us was in any shape to be discussing tonight. I stooped and picked up the blanket I'd dropped and draped it over her shoulders, then picked up a second one from a folded stack on the end of the fire truck's bumper. It was tantamount to theft, but if we were spending the rest of the night in St. Jude, we needed them more than the city did, if only to use as pillows. I could return them to Dawson when I saw her again.

"We'll talk later," I said. "After we sleep."

Phoenix nodded without question, trusting me as she had since she'd arrived at the Mary Magdalene, and together we made our way to St. Jude, leaving the emergency vehicles and personnel behind, along with the few remaining onlookers.

My newly developed paranoia, though? I swept my gaze over the otherwise empty night street one final time as I opened the driver's-side door and slid behind the wheel of the station wagon.

My paranoia came with me.

CHAPTER 17

"Sister Monica?"

Phoenix's soft voice came from the dark of the back seat, where she'd stretched out to sleep when I parked the car at the far end of a church parking lot. She'd wanted to give me the space, but I'd opted to remain in the driver's seat in case we needed to make a fast getaway. My body didn't appreciate the idea, but I doubted it would be much happier with St. Jude's back seat.

"Mm?" I answered, swatting at the high-pitched whine of a mosquito near my ear. We'd left the windows rolled down because of the heat, and unfortunately, the church bordered a large city park, which was a breeding ground for the voracious mini vampires. Only a few had found their way into the car so far, but there would undoubtedly be more.

I supposed I could have moved us to a different location, but that would have taken effort I didn't have the bandwidth for right now. Plus, despite my relationship with the church of my past, there was still something oddly reassuring about being near one. It was—

Phoenix's hand tapped my shoulder. "I forgot to give you this back."

I twisted around in my seat until I could see her hand and the glint of metal in it. My Mary Magdalene pendant —the one I'd take off and put on the porch railing before I'd gone to meet the intruder on the shelter's lawn. I couldn't believe I'd forgotten about it—then again, I supposed it wasn't that surprising, given life right now.

I reached up to take the pendant I'd worn for most of

my life—a gift from Mother Joan when I'd graduated from teaching college. Then I paused, and instead of taking the medal from Phoenix's palm, I folded her fingers over it.

"Keep it," I said. "She's been good to me. I want her to be good to you."

"Are you sure?"

"I'm sure."

Phoenix's fingers opened a little to give mine a squeeze, and then her hand disappeared back into the dark of the back seat and I returned to swatting mosquitoes.

"Sister Monica?" her voice came again.

"Mm?"

"Do you believe in God?"

My hand stilled in mid-flap. The question wasn't one I'd expected, but I supposed it wasn't surprising, either. Not in light of what she—we—had been through. I adjusted the blanket I'd folded up as a pillow between me and the car door, weighing my words with care, as I tried to straddle the fine line between my "complicated" truth and what I knew to be Phoenix's need for comfort and reassurance.

"I believe in a power higher than us, yes," I said.

"But not God."

"Not the same God that I was taught to believe in."

Phoenix was silent for a moment. Then, "Is that why you don't—didn't—have one of those cross things in your office?"

A smile tugged at my mouth. "A crucifix, you mean? I suppose that's one reason, yes."

"So … if you don't have one of those, what God do you believe in?"

"Are you sure you want to talk about this tonight? You should get some sleep."

"I've been trying, but every time I close my eyes—" Her voice caught, and I heard a tiny sniffle.

I twisted in my seat, ignoring the protests of my shoulder—and my spine, and my hips—and reached back to feel for her hand in the dark. Warm fingers curled around mine.

"I believe in a mother rather than a father, I think," I told her. "A wise woman who gave birth to our world and is watching over us as we grow up, but who knows that part of growing up means that we need to make our own mistakes and fix our own problems. Someone who loves us through those mistakes."

"You think God is a woman?" Phoenix sounded surprised.

"I think I like that idea more than a man who expects me to apologize all the time," I replied dryly. "Don't you?"

She giggled softly, then fell silent again, but she didn't let go of my hand. The city's night noises drifted in through the windows—vehicles passing by on the street beyond the stone half-wall that edged two sides of the parking lot, a distant siren, the *chirr* of crickets from the park.

Another damned mosquito.

"Sister Monica?"

"Yes, sweetheart?"

"Do you still pray?"

Hail Mary Magdalene, full of grace, come and sit with me.

I swallowed hard against the closing of my throat and the tears that wanted to fall again. Against the memories of burning homes and lost sisters and unprotected charges. Against the hole that had been torn in the very fabric of my world, and that of Phoenix.

Hail Mary Magdalene, sister to us all, come and pray for me …

"Sister?" Phoenix whispered.

I closed my eyes and squeezed her fingers. "All the time, Phoenix," I whispered back. "I pray all the time."

And never more than now.

By the time the city came to life in the morning, I'd texted Dawson with the number of the burner cell phone I'd acquired—which Phoenix told me made me "badass a.f."—and managed a whole three hours of pseudo sleep.

Pseudo because St. Jude's driver's seat really was *not* kind to my sixty-nine-year-old body, I'd been right about the whine of mosquitoes, and …

And the stone.

When I'd heard Phoenix's breathing deepen and even out in the seat behind me, I'd lifted my hips up until I could get my fingers into the pockets of my jeans—a task made more difficult by the sweltering weather that made everything, jeans included, sticky. I'd wriggled the flat rock out of its fabric sandwich with more determination than finesse, and then I'd taken a deep breath and opened my palm to study it.

Apart from showing the rock to Sister Ernestine and Detective Dawson, I hadn't had much time to look closely at it—hell, I hadn't *wanted* to look closely at it. I hadn't wanted it at all. But if I was going to be responsible for this thing until I found its rightful owner, I wanted to at least know more about it. I *needed* to know more.

Except there was nothing to see. I held the stone up and turned it this way and that, shone my new flip phone's flashlight onto it, ran my fingers over its every edge and surface, and learned nothing at all that I hadn't already known. It remained exactly what it had been before: flat, black, hard, and inanimate. It still had what looked like cobwebs embedded in it, and the webs were still attached to me.

The only … peculiarity, I suppose one could call it … was that nothing else seemed able to touch the webs that joined it to me. Or block them.

I noticed the anomaly when I set the stone on the dashboard behind the steering wheel in frustration and slumped back in my seat with my arms crossed and hands tucked beneath them. The sleeves of my shirt encased my arm, putting two layers of fabric plus the arm itself between the stone and my hand, and—

I stared at the fine, silver strands extending from the stone straight toward my arm. They definitely ended there, traveling neither under nor over the limb, but they also—I wriggled my fingers experimentally and felt the faint whisper of spider silk along them. Yup. They definitely remained there, as well.

I shivered and uncrossed my arms. The strands appeared full length again, glinting in the light from the phone sitting on the console beside me and stretching from stone to right hand. I passed my left hand through them. The filaments didn't so much as waver. Same when I picked up the cell phone and waved it over my hand. The web strands started at the stone and ended in my hand, as if they simply passed, undisturbed, through whatever stood between me and their source.

My flesh crawled at the thought, and I felt a sudden urge to just pitch the cursed thing out the window into the shrubbery. Even as my fingers twitched at the idea, however, a tiny, sharp pinch on my left arm distracted me. I smacked at it, then flicked away the remains of a mosquito from my stinging skin.

I turned a glare on the stone sitting on the dashboard. I was no wiser as to what it was, but like it or not—and cursed or not—it was mine for the moment. With a sigh, I stretched out my hand, picked it up, and re-pocketed it. Then I wadded up the remaining blanket, made myself as comfortable as I could against St. Jude's door, and settled down to a fitful sleep, broken by the multitude of thoughts crowding my mind: sheer, overwhelming, soul-devouring loss; dreams of fire and spiderwebs and giant cocoons …

And the question of what the hell I was going to do about Phoenix.

CHAPTER 18

I woke Phoenix at seven, when people began arriving
for early Mass. Several suspicious looks were being directed
at our vehicle in the parking lot, and we didn't need the
attention—or to have the police called on us. We took
turns going into the church to use the facilities, and then
Phoenix joined me in the front seat of the station wagon. I
turned the key in the ignition, St. Jude coughed and
hiccupped into life, and we joined the morning stop-and-
go traffic.

I headed for a diner that I knew served a cheap but
decent breakfast. We left the ungainly station wagon in a
parking garage a few streets away and walked—or, in my
case, limped—the short distance to the diner in silence. It
was good for my healing body to move, but the hours spent
in St. Jude had not been kind to me, and sweet Mary, I
hurt. Phoenix, bless her young heart, noted my hobble but
refrained from comment.

The diner was small—a dozen wooden booths and half
that many tables with mismatched chairs—and it was
already three-quarters filled with the pre-work crowd. For
an instant, I hesitated, wondering if it might be wiser to
use a drive-through. Then the lone server waved a coffee
pot in a vague invitation for us to seat ourselves, and the
intense desire to sit somewhere other than behind a
steering wheel overcame my misgivings. Besides, if they
hadn't found us in the church parking lot, it more than
likely meant they'd lost track of us altogether. At least
for now.

I chose a booth near the kitchen and—again—escape

through the back, if we needed it, then took the seat facing the door. We both ordered coffee, eggs, and toast, sat mostly in silence while we waited for the arrival of our food and avoided talking about the herd of elephants in the room, and then—

And then, as we picked at our cooling meals, I told Phoenix what I'd decided about her in the pale light of dawn. She was not pleased by my idea—or remotely cooperative.

"No." She slammed her mug down on the worn, pale blue laminate tabletop between us. "Absolutely not."

I plucked a handful of napkins from the metal dispenser and reached across to mop up the coffee that had slopped out of her cup. My shoulder gave an audible crack. It might not have been broken, but it was still far from happy.

"I know it's not ideal—" I said.

She cut me off. "Are you kidding? It's fucking crap. Another shelter? Seriously? Do you know what those places are like?"

I did, and I wished I had another alternative, but I didn't, and so I pushed on, because I had to. For her sake and for mine.

"But it's better than going back to the street," I continued, setting the sodden wad of napkins aside. "You'll have a roof over your head, food—"

"No."

"—and you can continue your hormone therapy," I finished, dropping my voice. I extended my hand toward hers, but she pulled away and tucked both of hers out of sight in her lap. I sighed. "Phoenix, please. Try to understand. I need to know that you're okay. That you're somewhere safe, and—"

"Then take me with you."

"I don't even know where *I'm* going," I said, "and even if I did, and even if we could guarantee continuing your treatments, you and I both know that being with me isn't what either of us would call 'safe.' Not right now. Not until I figure out what I've gotten myself into."

Phoenix crossed her arms over her chest in a gesture that I suspected was part stubborn and part defensive. Behind her scowl, however, the look on her face was all vulnerability, and her voice was small. "I don't want to go into a shelter."

"I know, sweetie. And it's the last thing I want for you, too, but we honestly have no choice." I motioned to the server for our bill, and he nodded acknowledgment. Phoenix's breakfast was only half-eaten, and mine less so, but I didn't think either of us had much appetite for more right now. I turned my attention back to her while we waited.

"I'll at least make some calls, and we'll go from there, all right? Can we at least agree on that?"

Arms still crossed, she stared out the window beside our booth. "Whatever."

The server appeared tableside and set the bill beside my new cell phone, promising to return with the card machine in a moment. I extracted one of the bank cards from my back pocket in readiness, searching for words of reassurance to share with Phoenix, but I had none for her.

Hell, I didn't think I had any for myself.

I glanced at the darkened display on the phone. I'd still heard nothing from Detective Sergeant Dawson. How long did it take to check the system for a missing person, anyway? I wished I'd thought to ask. And that I'd emphasized the urgency. Not that she was likely to have missed that after last night's—

The phone on the table rang and vibrated at the same

time, making both me and Phoenix jump. I grabbed for it and flipped it open as the server returned to the table with the card machine.

"Detec—" I began, because Dawson was the only person it could be.

Her terse voice cut me off. "Did you get your burner phone at a convenience store on Wellesley last night?"

"What?"

The server glanced down at the bill on the table and began punching numbers into the machine.

"Wellesley," Dawson repeated. "Did you get the phone at a store on Wellesley?"

"I—" I scrunched up my forehead in thought, trying to remember. Everything after leaving the internet café seemed hazy, but—"I think so?"

"Did you use your bank card?"

"Yes, why?" I picked up said card as the server set the machine on the table and turned it toward me.

"Did you use the same card at the internet café?"

"What is this about?" I checked the machine total against the bill, added a tip, and selected the savings account option.

"*Did you use it at the internet café?*" She bit out the question a second time, her tone demanding an answer.

I stared at the card I held, my grip on it tightening as cold fingers of apprehension wrapped around my gut. "Yes. Yes, I did. What the hell is going on, Detective?"

"Where are you now?"

"Just about to pay for breakfast."

"All right. Listen carefully." She took a deep breath at the other end of the line, then, her voice calm and even, said, "The store you got the phone at was destroyed in a fire last night. The clerk is in critical condition. Someone beat the shit out of him to get the information they wanted

—on you. They have your vehicle description, and I think they might be tracking your bank card."

The edges of the card bit into my hand, and I stared across the table at Phoenix. Sweet, vulnerable Phoenix, who stared back at me, her eyes wide with questions—and fear. My responsibility for her settled like lead across my shoulders and panic—like more lead, only molten—into my chest. I forced my attention back to Dawson's voice.

"Sister? Are you still there?"

"I'm here," I said. "What do I do? Not including coming in to you."

"Where are you parked? Anywhere near where you are?"

"No. A parking garage a few blocks away."

"Good. Tell me the name of the restaurant, and then have another coffee. I'll come to you. With cash."

I picked up the bill from the table, read off the name of the diner to her, and started to give her the address. She cut me off.

"I know it," she said. "I'll be there in ten minutes."

CHAPTER 19

Waiting for the police detective to arrive was the longest ten minutes of my life.

Dawson actually made it there in eight and a half, according to the clock above the kitchen door, but in those minutes, I envisioned and died a thousand deaths.

Worse, I envisioned those deaths for Phoenix.

I'd sent the server away, telling him that a friend would be joining us for a while, and that we would pay afterward. His gaze had flashed between me and Phoenix—it would have been impossible not to have sensed the tension at the table—but he'd shrugged and canceled the transaction on the machine.

"No worries," he'd said. "Just let me know when you're ready."

Phoenix had waited until he was out of earshot before pointing at my white-knuckled hand with my bank card peeking out at the edges. "That's how they found us at the internet café?"

Her question told me she'd heard at least some of my conversation with Dawson, and I'd forced my hand to relax and set the card on the table between us. Its outline remained as angry red lines etched on my palm and the tender pads of my fingers.

"Yes," I'd confirmed.

She'd exhaled a shaky breath. "Tracking a bank card is some seriously high-level shit," she'd said. "You know that, right?"

"I suspected."

"Like cop-level shit."

I'd suspected that, too, and knew what she was intimating. But while trusting Dawson might be—was—a risk, we had few other options. Not now that we were without money, couldn't chance returning to our vehicle, and still had idea where we were going.

Where *I* was going, I corrected myself again. Whether she liked it or not, Phoenix could not, would not, be coming with me. Not because I was afraid of the responsibility—heaven knew I was no stranger to that—but because leaving her behind *was* the responsible thing to do. As much as I dreaded being alone, I dreaded more that I might see her die in one of the scenarios I kept imagining.

The diner's front door swung open, and Dawson stepped inside, wearing the same suit she'd had on at the internet café and carrying a brown paper bag. She removed her sunglasses and scanned the crowded interior, looking like she'd had about as much sleep as I'd had. I raised my hand to get her attention, and her sharp gaze zeroed in on me.

She threaded her way between tables to our booth and, arriving, pointed at Phoenix. "Put your hood up and move over," she ordered. Then she pulled a Toronto Blue Jays baseball cap from the bag and handed it to me, along with the sunglasses she'd taken off. "Put these on."

Neither of us questioned her directives. Phoenix flipped up the hood on her sweatshirt, hiding her face within its depths; I settled the baseball cap on my head—the first time in my life that I'd ever worn one—and settled the sunglasses onto my nose. The world dimmed by half.

Satisfied, Dawson slid onto the booth seat beside Phoenix, waited until the server poured coffee into a cup for her, waved off the breakfast menu, and then waited some more until he departed. Then she inflated her cheeks and blew out a puff of air.

"Well, shit," she said.

It was not what I was hoping she'd lead with.

"How is the convenience store clerk?" I asked. "Have you heard anything more?"

"Not yet, no."

"Is it cops?" Phoenix asked from the depths of her hood. "Tracking the bank card, I mean."

Dawson regarded her sideways. "Maybe," she allowed. "But there could be another explanation, too. The fact that we caught on so soon is in our favor. We need to focus on that, and on keeping you both safe." She nodded at the bank card still lying on the table. "How much do you have in your account?"

"I honestly have no idea," I said. "That one is from the Sisters of St. Mary. Sister Ernestine gave it to me yesterday, when—" Phoenix flinched, and I broke off, reframing my thoughts to avoid the immediate past. Then, unlocking my jaw, I continued, "I was going to take cash out and check the balance when I got the cell phone last night, but the ATM was out of order."

"You said *that one*. You have another?"

I pulled the other bank card from my pocket and set it beside the first. "This one is for the household account for the Mary Magdalene. There should be five hundred dollars available." That much I was sure of, thanks to sweating—and swearing—over the ledgers.

"Less the cost of the milk I bought yesterday," Phoenix reminded me, her voice catching. "Eight dollars and forty-three cents."

Brief sympathy flashed in Dawson's eyes, but she shrugged it off with a twitch of one shoulder and returned to business. Apparently she, too, felt our time crunch.

"Is there a limit to what you can withdraw in one day?" she asked.

"A thousand on the household account, I think, when there's that much available. I'm not sure about the other. Sister Ernestine handled the sister house finances."

"Right." She dug a hand into a pocket of the blazer she wore and pulled out a wad of cash. "There's two grand there. It probably won't get you very far, but it's all I have on hand at the moment, so it will have to do. I'll take the cards and the passwords and withdraw the same amount, then hold onto the cards for you until—well. Until."

I raised startled eyes from the cash she held out to me and shook my head. "Detective Dawson, I can't let you—"

"Sister Monica," she said, cutting across my objection. "You have no choice. You need to get to St. Paul's, and whatever that thing is that you're carrying"—she nodded across the table, her gaze dropping to where the stone nestled in my pocket—"it's not a transporter."

"Wait, what? Get where?" I gaped in return.

"St. Paul's—" She stopped and shook her head, her mouth compressing. "Shit. I didn't tell you yet, did I? I found Sister Margaret's name in the system. She was reported missing by the Mother Superior at St. Paul's Monastery in Kingston a little over six months ago."

Six months—St. Paul's—Kingston—

My mind bounced between the details Dawson had rattled off, and I reeled at the information. The possibilities. The *im*possibilities. I remembered a Sister Margaret there—could it really have been her? But how? Surely I would have recognized—

A full-color image of the skeletal woman on the porch flashed across my memory, and I shuddered. She had hardly been recognizable as human, let alone as someone I had once known. Someone from a lifetime ago. I put an elbow on the table and pressed my fingertips against my lips, digesting the news.

Its impact.

The horror behind it.

"Sister?" Phoenix stretched out a hand to touch my arm. "Are you okay? You look like you just saw a ghost."

I dredged up what I hoped was a smile but felt more like a grimace and patted her hand in reassurance. "I'm —" I began, but then I stopped, because *fine*? I was anything but. My shoulders sagged, and I looked out the window at the street beyond, darkened by my new sunglasses. By my heart.

"I'm a little shocked," I said more truthfully, my voice gruff. "I think I knew Sister Margaret. St. Paul's Monastery is—" I took a deep breath and finished in a rush, "It's where I took my vows."

CHAPTER 20

Four more cups of coffee—each—were consumed while we hashed out the best plan for getting me to Kingston and St. Paul's. And while I wrapped my head around the idea of *going* back.

I'd never thought I would.

In some ways, leaving the monastery itself had been even harder than leaving the church. Between my time as a novitiate and then as a nun, I'd spent almost thirty years inside the stone walls. It had been home, and the women I'd shared it with had been my family. Or at least, I'd thought they'd been.

But my decision to leave the church had taken away not only my calling and my home, but my sisters, too, because it felt as if they had turned their collective backs on me when I had left. It had been inevitable. I'd known it would happen as soon as our Mother Superior had made it clear that neither my ideas nor I were welcome any longer —and when the archbishop had backed her decision. Mother Annunciata had refused to allow me to say goodbye, and I had been too indoctrinated—and too grief-stricken by my expulsion—to even contemplate standing up to her.

I'd felt like I was running away, leaving under the cover of darkness that February night, with no word to any of them. And no word *from* them, either, because Mother Annunciata's rule over the monastery had been …

Well. *Controversial* would have been the kindest way to describe it. I often wondered whether a part of her had feared an exodus in my wake, but I suspected that a greater part hadn't been able to bear the thought of watching the others say their farewells to me. We had been a close-knit community, despite the wedges she'd tried to drive between us. Or perhaps because of them.

And now I was going back.

"Earth to Sister Monica."

Phoenix's voice penetrated my scattered thoughts, and I jolted back to the present.

"Sorry," I said. "I was …"

"Already in Kingston?" Detective Dawson hazarded, adding another packet of sugar to her—in my opinion— already too-sweet coffee. The woman really did like her sugar, didn't she?

"Unfortunately," I agreed.

Dawson stirred the coffee. "Not an easy parting of ways?"

"It never is, when excommunication is involved."

Astute brown eyes narrowed a fraction. "You left the church, too? Not just the convent?"

"The church left me," I corrected. "My actions"—in great part, my activism on women's and LGBTQIA+ rights—"were deemed incompatible with their teachings." So had been my rejection of the punitive God that they preached, but that was a whole other story. One that Phoenix appeared to think I needed to share, because—

"Sister Monica thinks God is a woman," she volunteered.

Dawson raised an eyebrow at her. "Does she, now," she murmured. Then to me, she said, "And you didn't want to change?"

I snorted. "*They* didn't want to change," I corrected her. I told myself to stop there, before I got up on my soap box, but I'd never been very good at keeping my words to myself. I shrugged irritably.

"Let's face it," I heard my tart voice continue, "the church is the ultimate patriarchy. When I was young and idealistic, I thought that I might help to change that from the inside—or at least influence it. I was wrong."

A tiny smile quirked at the side of Dawson's mouth. "I think I like you, Sister Monica."

"Thank you," I said. "I like me, too. Now, I'm assuming I can't use St. Jude now that they have its description, so any ideas about how I'm supposed to get to the monastery?"

Dawson looked blank for a second, then her expression cleared. "The car," she remembered. "Leave it where it is. You can use mine."

The suggestion surprised me, and I shook my head. "I can't—"

"You can, because it's the only way. You have to give your name to get a bus or train ticket these days, and we don't know how wide their surveillance net extends. I'll tell the department my personal vehicle is in for repairs. They'll let me use my work one." Taking my agreement for granted, she slid a key fob across the table toward me. "I'll walk you to where I'm parked, and we'll pick up a new burner for you on the way."

"But I already have one."

"Burners can be tracked. The fact this place is still standing"—she tipped her head to indicate the diner surrounding us—"likely means they haven't been able to do so *yet*, but we're not taking any chances. We'll dump the one you have in a garbage can." She drained her coffee cup and set it on the table.

"So," she said briskly, "the plan, such as it is: dump your phone, get a new burner, take my car to St. Paul's in Kingston, call me when you get there, and let me know what you find out about Sister Margaret. Then we decide on your next step. Anything else before I get the bill?"

It was more of a plan than I'd had before this, but I still hesitated. My gaze, heavy with guilt and grief and sadness, settled on Phoenix. "Yes," I said. "There's one more thing. Phoenix needs somewhere to stay."

The young woman who had been sitting quietly beside the detective shrank further into her hoodie as—with as few words as possible, because she flinched at every one of them—I explained her situation to Dawson. To my infinite relief and gratitude, the cop listened—and more importantly, heard.

"So," she said when I finished. "No shelters, then."

"That would be preferable," I agreed. I would have liked to reach across the table to Phoenix, but her hands were tucked out of sight in her lap. "But going through social services will take—"

"An eternity. I know." Dawson gave Phoenix a narrow, sideways look. "Apart from that internet café stunt, you've been keeping your hands clean? No hacking, no unauthorized access?" Her questions made it clear that she'd familiarized herself with my young companion's record.

Phoenix scowled at her in return. "Of course," she snapped. "If I hadn't, Sister Monica would never have let me stay at—with—" She broke off and looked away, biting at the ring in her bottom lip and blinking back tears that only I could see.

"And I won't, either," said Dawson. "So let's make sure we're clear on that, shall we?"

"I don't understand," I said.

The detective sighed and grimaced as she half-turned in her seat to face Phoenix, who was eyeing her warily again. "I have an apartment over my garage," she told the young woman. "It's not much, and you'll need to give it a good cleaning because it hasn't been used in a decade or more, but you'll be safe there."

Both of us stared at her in astonishment—me, at Dawson's level of generosity; Phoenix, at the unexpected trust being shown in her by, of all people, a cop.

"You'd do that?" Her expression narrowed in suspicion. "Why? You don't even know me."

"I have excellent instincts," Dawson replied. "It's my superpower."

"Won't your husband object?"

"I'm divorced. No kids. It's just me and my cats—three of them. Which reminds me: one cat lady crack, and you're out."

Phoenix looked across at me, her expression a jumble of doubt, wistfulness, and fear. Fear of being left behind, of losing me, of letting someone new—someone like the no-nonsense Dawson, cat-lady jokes aside—into her bubble.

Summoning a reassurance I didn't actually feel, I smiled at her in return, past the hollowness in my chest, past my blooming loneliness, past my own fear that I might never see her again, either.

"So?" Dawson asked. "Yes or no?"

"Yes," I accepted on Phoenix's behalf. "And thank you."

And then I watched a single tear slide down Phoenix's cheek.

CHAPTER 21

Phoenix's single tear stayed with me for the entire three-and-a-half-hour drive from Toronto to the outskirts of Kingston. There had been no others. Not when I'd hugged her stiff, unresponsive frame, not when I'd climbed into Detective Dawson's sensible four-door sedan—of an equally sensible and nondescript gray-blue color—and not when I'd glanced in the rearview mirror as I'd pulled away and left her standing on the sidewalk beside the police detective.

On the other hand, one tear had been all that was needed, guaranteeing that I would reconsider my decision to leave the young woman behind more times than I could count—and that I would nearly turn back to get her at least a half a dozen of those times. Deep in my gut, however, I knew I'd been right to leave her with Dawson. And not just *with* Dawson, but in the cop's care, because as she'd given me a rundown on how her far-more-modern-than-St.-Jude vehicle functioned, the detective had paused and looked me in the eye, her brown gaze steady.

"I'll look after her," she said. "You have my word."

I'd nodded back, my throat too tight to speak, and without missing another beat, Dawson had gone back to explaining how the cruise control and something called "driver assistance" worked. Staring out the windshield at Phoenix, my last connection to what I'd begun to think of as my own personal pre-stone age, I hadn't heard a word.

And now … now I was here. Three and a half hours— well, two and a half if you didn't take the convoluted, clumsily evasive route that I'd driven—away from that life and about to step back into the one I'd left twenty-two years before.

I should definitely have turned back.

I still could, of course, except that would solve nothing. The answers I needed weren't in Toronto; they were here. At least, I hoped they were here, although frankly, I was at a loss as to how they could be. The stone I carried and the monastery I'd left had about as much in common as me and the church I'd defied.

I stood at the wrought-iron gates, staring through them at the wide, crushed-stone driveway beyond and the building at its end. Set back a hundred yards from the quiet street that it occupied on Kingston's outskirts, the monastery was two stories high, built of limestone, and as imposing now as I remembered it.

Towering maples shaded the building and the sweep of lawn that surrounded it—a sweep of lawn that looked smaller than I remembered, as if it were slowly being swallowed by the forest that covered the remainder of the fifteen-acre property.

Once, I'd treasured walks through the woods, but now they looked as foreboding as the building. I shivered and lifted my gaze to the monastery's second floor, where each bare window marked a small bedroom. Mine had been the third from the left, and I wondered briefly who occupied it now. In my novice days, there had been curtains. But a new Mother Superior had been installed a year after I took my vows, and all the curtains had disappeared along with everything else that she had considered "soft."

Down duvets had been replaced by rough wool blankets, flowers had disappeared from garden beds turned entirely over to vegetables, we had gone back to wearing the habits that had once been traditional to our order, and the few small strides we'd made in standing up to the church's patriarchy had been ruthlessly squashed—by a woman who should have been one of our own.

I would never understand that, how a woman could uphold her own oppression. How she could willingly, passionately subjugate herself to the power plays of men— not to mention throw her fellow women under the wheels of the same bus.

And the fact that the monastery's population had more than doubled not just since Mother Annunciata's arrival, but because of it?

That just blew my mind.

I sent a last, wistful glance toward the sedan I'd parked a block away, then sent a more baleful one at the lawn across the street to where a ceramic garden gnome had been watching my state of stasis with a grin that was entirely too cheerful. I scowled back at him, then pulled my shoulders back and turned away to tug on the bell rope that would summon someone to open the gate.

It was time to beard the lion in her den.

Mother Annunciata did not disappoint.

The nun who admitted me at the gate took me as far as the entry hall, where she left me standing while she went in search of her superior. I was pretty sure that the length of time I was kept waiting was due to the name I'd given: Sister Monica Barrett from the Mary Magdalene House for Women.

Scratch that. I was entirely sure.

I probably should have dropped the *sister* title, under the circumstances. It would have been wiser to appease St. Paul's Mother Superior than knowingly antagonize her when I'd come looking for help. On the other hand, I was fiercely attached to the title I'd held onto, and just as fiercely glad that I'd used it. Mother Annunciata would never see it as anything other than an act of defiance, but it had been my identity—with or without the church—for most of my life. Now, after losing both the shelter that had been my calling and the sister house that had been my home, it was all I had left.

I was all I had left.

And I was damned if I'd let Mother Misery take it from me.

Ten minutes became twenty, and twenty became thirty, all marked by the loud ticking of the grandfather clock sitting beside the foot of the stairs. I stopped beside it on my forty-third tour of the hallway—because, apparently, creature comforts such as chairs for callers had also been done away with by Mother Annunciata—and ran a gentle hand over the polished wood.

An unexpected rush of nostalgia filled me. It had been my job to wind the clock once a week during my novitiate, something I always did before the others woke and the day started. There had been something rare and precious about being up at four-thirty to commune with the old clock, something … timeless, despite my task being a timepiece. I missed that.

I swallowed against the lump in my throat. Sometimes, I missed a lot of things about the monastery—at least as it had been when I'd joined. The camaraderie. The simplicity of the routine. The safety and protection afforded by the stone walls and my vocation. The world had seemed a harsh place when I'd first left St. Paul's, and it had taken me a long time to be able to look beyond that harshness to the beauty, and to stop being at war with it.

It had taken a longer time to stop being at war with myself—a battle I still found myself fighting some days, when my doubts and insecurities whispered that it would have been easier to remain part of the fold. Or when nostalgia for my lost community made the back of my throat burn the way it did now.

I swallowed hard and, to distract myself, let my gaze pan the hallway yet again, taking in its austerity and focusing on changes that I might have missed. There honestly weren't many, apart from the missing chairs. Dark wood stairs sat to the right of the clock, polished and impeccably maintained, with grooves worn into their treads by thousands of footsteps. Four closed doors broke the stark, white-walled perimeter, all of wood as dark as the stairs, blocking curious eyes and barring uninvited access to the private spaces beyond.

One of the doors led to the kitchen and dining room, one to a wing of main-floor bedrooms for those with limited mobility, a third into a sitting room kept for rare family visits, and the fourth, with an ornate crucifix hanging above it, opened into—

I gave a start when, as if on cue, the door swung open, and a tall, broad woman—as austere as the monastery she ruled over—stood in the opening.

Chapter 22

For a long moment, Mother Annunciata and I stared at one another without speaking: she, likely because she was waiting for me to say something first; I, because I couldn't have forced words through my clenched teeth if my life had depended on it. I finally inclined my head in what I hoped would appear as a gesture of respect, even though it was more to hide my expression and give myself time to quash the—anger, distaste, disgust?—that flared in me.

Probably all three, I admitted to myself. I took a deep breath, remembered why I was here, and raised my gaze again to the glacier-blue one. Slowly, her expression giving away nothing, Mother Annunciata looked me over from head to toe and back again before, still without a word, she stood back for me to enter her office.

The lion's den.

I walked past her to stand in the center of the room. That hadn't changed in my absence, either. The same desk sat in the same spot in front of the same window—curtainless, of course—with another crucifix above it. The same bookshelves lined the walls, laden with obscure theological texts, the only books the sisters were allowed to read. A single hard, straight-backed chair sat on this side of the desk for visitors, and another hard, wooden chair sat behind the desk. That one, at least, had armrests.

It was also on casters, I remembered, which allowed the occupant to shove the chair dramatically backward and thrust herself upright when the occasion called for an extra dose of intimidation. Such as the night she'd stood and shoved a paper grocery bag at me, ordered me to change into the clothes it held, and informed me that I would be leaving immediately.

The impulse to turn and depart again was almost overwhelming. I might have done so but for the faint tickle of spiderwebs across the back of my hand. I curled my fingers into a fist, drew myself up tall, and forced my rigid shoulders down from my ears, willing myself to hold my ground.

Sister Margaret, I reminded myself. *You're here for Margaret.*

And for the stone.

I watched from the corner of my eye as Mother Annunciata closed the door and glided across the hardwood floor to her desk. Her feet didn't make a sound. They never had, giving her the uncanny ability to be anywhere and everywhere with no warning whatsoever, ensuring that no one dared speak out of turn lest she overhear. It was one of the reasons her reign over the monastery had been —and still was, I felt sure—one of fear rather than respect.

Briefly, I wondered what had made her the way she was. I'd seen enough in my years on the outside to know that humankind was fragile at best, and that cruelty all too often stemmed from monsters in one's own past. On the other hand, I'd also seen enough to know that wasn't the case for everyone. And I wasn't here to figure out which scenario applied in Annunciata's case.

Mother Annunciata lowered herself into the wooden chair, which didn't dare squeak beneath her not-inconsequential weight, and tilted back in it. Resting her elbows on the armrests, she steepled her fingers against her chin.

"Monica," she said.

"Mother," I replied. I almost gagged on the title, but again, this was her territory, and I was the one in need of help. Or at least information. "I've come about Sist—"

"No."

I blinked in consternation. "I beg your pardon?"

"You left, Monica. You are no longer a part of this community, and as such, I cannot in good faith share informa—"

"Margaret," I said, cutting across her pomposity. Her tone had actually been quite gentle, the kind one might use when reasoning with an uncooperative child, but paired with the icy, disdainful gaze? Oh, it was pomposity, all right. And Sister Margaret's name had cut it off at its knees.

"You reported her missing," I said. "Six months ago."

Mother Annunciata's mouth tightened into a thin line. She hated this. Hated that I might have information that she wanted. It was in my power to make her squirm, but tempting though the idea might be, I would not. In part because I needed to know about Margaret, but mostly because of me. Because I was not and never would be anything like the Mother Superior—or like the father she had always reminded me of.

On the other hand, waiting for her to ask for the information was only polite, right?

"You have news of her?" Mother Annunciata asked at last, settling the chair back down to level and resting her hands, now linked, on the desk between us.

"She's dead." I winced at my bluntness. I hadn't meant to be quite so direct, but neither was I sure how else to frame my news. I'd never cared for terms that tried to be delicate. *Passed on, no longer with us, gone to her Savior.* Humanity had created many ways to dance around the topic of death, but when it came down to it, dead was dead, and prettifying the announcement never made it any easier.

On this, at least, Mother Annunciata and I seemed to

be in agreement, because she didn't so much as blink at the news.

"I see," she said. "When?"

I had to think about that for a moment, because so much had happened that it felt like a week or more, but it had only been—I calculated rapidly, recalculated because no, that couldn't be right, and then answered, "The day before yesterday."

"You sound uncertain."

"Shocked that it was *only* the day before yesterday, perhaps," I said, "but no. I'm certain." And the time-frame explained a lot, when I thought about it. Like why I was so damned tired—my sleepless night and drive from Toronto aside. I sent a longing glance at the straight-backed chair on my side of the desk. I'd been subjected to it often enough to know that it was the antithesis of comfortable, but right now? It looked as soft as a cloud.

"Well," said Mother Annunciata. "Well."

I caved to my yearning and opened my mouth to ask if I could sit to answer her questions and ask my own, but before I'd uttered a sound, she rose to her feet. The chair rolled a few inches back without particular dramatic flair, and the Mother Superior of St. Paul's Monastery floated soundlessly across the room to open the door she'd closed behind me scant moments before.

"Thank you for coming to tell me," she said. "I will pass the news on to the others at dinner."

Sheer incredulity—and probably a return of the long-ingrained obedience that I thought I'd shed—carried me halfway out the door before I managed to put the brakes on and turn back to her. A mere two feet separated us, and I gripped the doorframe to steady myself against the determined energy that radiated from her, pushing me out.

"That's it?" I asked. "You don't want to know what happened? How she died? How I know about it?"

"I do not," Mother Annunciata replied, her voice turning as cold as her eyes had remained. "Sister Margaret chose to leave our sanctum without either word or permission. I made the report as a matter of law, nothing more. She made her choices, and the consequences of those choices have no bearing here."

Heat unfurled in my belly at the lack of compassion, the callousness. Whatever might have happened in Annunciata's past did not excuse this. It could never excuse this. I took a step toward her, closing the space between us.

The Mother Superior was taller than me by six inches and broader by a good deal more, but somehow I managed to look down my nose at her all the same, channeling all of my disgust into the most withering gaze that I could summon as I bit out the accusations I'd bottled up inside myself for more than two decades.

"You, Mother Annunciata," I said with quiet but utter conviction, "are the heart and soul of what is wrong with this entire church. Your holier-than-thou attitude, your grasping control over those you're supposed to lead, your fucking *blind* obedience to the ones who control *you*. You and everyone like you, who pay lip service to loving your Lord but wouldn't know real love if it slapped you across the face. How dare you? How *dare* you take the teachings of the man you claim as the Son of God and twist them to suit yourselves and only yourselves?"

I stopped for breath, hating that I was shaking with my own fury. No. Not fury. Impotence. Because none of what I said mattered—or ever would matter—to the woman before me, or to any of the pious. I had achieved nothing in the twenty-five years I'd spent here. Not change, not impact, nothing.

And now, I didn't even have the answers I'd come looking for. I still knew nothing of Sister Margaret or the stone or—

"Are you quite done?" Annunciata inquired without inflection of any kind. Twenty-two years ago, her tone would have cowed me into submission. Now, it just made me tired and angry and—

A flicker of movement caught my eye on the other side of Annunciata's office, and I shifted my gaze past her shoulder to a gap in the bookcase-lined wall—and a face barely visible in the shadows of that gap. An old nun, her face wreathed in wrinkles, held a single finger to her lips in caution, then tilted her head to the left in silent invitation before the gap closed again. I blinked once in astonishment, again as I swiftly processed this new development, and a third time as I steeled myself to look back up at Annunciata.

"I am, actually," I replied wearily. "In fact, I'm beyond done. You're not going to change, Annunciata. Not now and not ever, because you don't want to change. For reasons I cannot begin to fathom, you *choose* to be this way, and I just hope you're ready for the consequences of your own choices."

Whether it was my lack of respect in dropping her *Mother* title or my throwing the idea of *consequences* back in her face, I would never know. Either way, I'd cracked the cold, controlled facade at last. Her face twisting with an ugliness that came from deep inside her, Annunciata raised both hands toward my chest. I could have easily blocked her, but instead I stepped back, depriving her of the push she so wanted to deliver.

She staggered and caught herself only by grabbing the doorframe. If it hadn't been for the phone ringing in her office, she might have taken a second run at me. Instead, she hesitated, spat something unintelligible at me, and slammed her office door in my face. I stared at the dark wood for a moment before wiping the spittle from my cheek, then turned toward the hallway—

And the ancient nun leaning on a cane in the shadow of the old clock, waiting for me.

Chapter 23

Her name was Sister Anne Louise, I learned, and she'd come to St. Paul's two years after I'd left. And for a woman who had at least twenty years on me, she moved with astonishing speed.

I was hard pressed to keep pace with the tapping of her cane as she bolted through the door and down the narrow hallway leading to the main-floor living quarters. She'd introduced herself in a whisper as the grandfather clock chimed five, marking the call to Vespers, told me she would take me somewhere we could talk, and then seized my arm above the elbow and propelled me along with her.

When we heard footsteps approaching around a corner ahead of us, she opened a door and thrust me into a bare, unoccupied cell, then followed me in and pressed a finger to her wrinkled lips. I didn't need to be told twice. We stood in silence until the footsteps passed. No voices accompanied them. St. Paul's wasn't a silent order, but Annunciata demanded quiet at all times in the corridors—as well as in the gardens, dining room, and kitchen. Which left only the sitting room where we—*they*—gathered in the evenings after dinner for conversation that could be closely monitored by a certain Mother Superior.

I put my ear to the door, but I could hear nothing more. The hall outside was silent. "They've gone," I whispered to Sister Anne Louise, "but won't you be missed at Vespers?"

The ancient nun snorted. "Advanced age needs to come with *some* perks," she said. "I've been excused from that woman's impossible schedule ever since I turned ninety-nine and told the bishop that I just couldn't keep up with it anymore."

The idea of her being ninety-nine warred with my skepticism over her limitations, because I recognized a powerhouse when I met one.

"That was two years ago," she added, opening the door a crack and peering into the corridor. "I've rather enjoyed sleeping in, I won't lie. Those four-thirty mornings for Lauds are the work of the devil, if you ask me, but we're not here to talk about the vagaries of my calling, and we're almost there. Now, come."

Without further preamble, she opened the door, checked the corridor in both directions, then scurried from the room, her cane tapping rhythmically against the tile floor. Wrestling now with the hundred and one idea, I followed.

We traveled to the end, then turned left and stopped in front of a door that, if my memory served, opened onto a set of stairs leading down to a death-trap of a cellar.

I'd only ever seen it once, when Annunciata had assigned me and another of the sisters to clean it for use as storage. Given the size of the building and the number of empty closets and rooms that existed, the idea had been preposterous—and her true intention of punishing me and Sister Rose transparently obvious.

No one had said anything to her, however. No one had dared. So Sister Rose and I had descended the rickety stairs with buckets and mops in hand—only to have Sister Rose go through the rotted, second-to-last tread, break her ankle, and be taken away in an ambulance. I could still hear the poor girl's screams.

Even Annunciata had drawn the line at risking a second mishap, and so the buckets had been left behind, the door had been locked, and as far as I knew, neither the incident nor the cellar had ever been mentioned again. Until now.

"It's safe," Sister Anne Louise assured me, patting my arm. "It's always been safe. You just need to know where to step."

I would have liked more details on the *always* part, but she'd turned away again and was fumbling with a key, trying to insert it into the lock. Just as I reached to help, there was a metallic click, a satisfied, "Ha!" from Sister Anne Louise, and then a squeal of hinges in need of oiling.

Instinctively, I looked back the way we'd come. The corridor remained empty, however, and I turned back to my companion ... who was nowhere to be seen.

"Close the door behind you," her voice called up from the black hole facing me. "It's best to hug the wall—the stairs are more solid on that side."

As versus having one collapse beneath me, breaking *my* ankle?

Awesome.

Taking a deep breath, I shuffled forward into a darkness that seemed determined to swallow even the faintest light. I closed the door behind me as instructed, and then, following the rest of Sister Anne Louise's instructions, leaned against the wall to my left and gingerly descended into the even darker dark—all while trying not to think about the spiders and other interesting creatures I was almost certainly collecting along the way. The webs from the stone were bad enough, but actual webs from actual spiders were a whole other level of *hell no* in my mind.

My foot settled onto a surface different from the wooden steps, and I slid the toe of my shoe forward cautiously. It met with no edge or drop-off. I'd reached the bottom, but where was—

A light flared, and I threw a hand up against it.

Blinking away the spots, I made out Sister Anne Louise's stooped form on the other side of the dank, clutter-filled cellar, where she was lighting a lantern hanging on the wall. She replaced the lantern's glass mantle over the flame, which brightened and then settled into a steady glow. The nun blew out the match she held and dropped it to the floor. Then she turned to face me, gripped the shaft of her cane in her left hand and the handle with her right, and pulled a long, tapered sword free of it.

She lunged.

Two decades of martial arts training and two black belts reacted before I'd even registered my astonishment. I took a swift, defensive step back, putting enough distance between me and Sister Anne Louise to throw off her attack. The elderly nun wobbled but recovered faster than I expected, and I—

I tripped over the buckets that were still in the cellar after three decades.

Perhaps if I hadn't been sore and exhausted, I might have recovered my footing. As it was, though, my arms flew wide in a search for balance, my shoulder gave an almighty twinge that traveled from jaw to hip bone, and I was done. I crashed to the floor amid buckets, accompanying mops, and scattered bits of abandoned furniture.

"Sweet Mary Magdalene," I wheezed when the clatter abated, and I found my breath again. And then I wheezed again for an entirely different reason, because the sword in Sister Anne Louise's hand now had its tip resting against my throat.

My gaze traced the long, polished glint of metal back to the nun's steady grip, then lifted to meet hers. There wasn't a lot of light from the lantern, but it was enough to see the unflinching determination behind her expression—

and the assurance that she knew how to use the weapon she held and wouldn't hesitate to do so.

I didn't dare so much as swallow.

"Good," the old nun said, nodding satisfaction. "We understand one another. Now, who are you, and what the hell happened to Margaret? And remember, no one comes down here. Ever. So if I don't like your answers, it will be a long, long time before your body is found."

Well. That was clear enough.

I stared up at her, swiftly weighing my choices—and my odds. Both seemed pretty slim. Even if I did manage to overpower her—and that was a big *if*, given the pressure of the blade against my skin and a spasm threatening to take hold in my back—doing so would put me right back to square one, with no more answers than I'd had when I arrived. Answers I was certain Sister Anne Louise had but wouldn't share, unless I gave her reason to.

"Fine," I said. "But can I at least sit up first?"

Sister Anne Louise regarded me for a second, then nodded and took a step back, taking the blade with her but keeping it between us. She'd been well trained, just as sisters Ernestine and Helen had been. What the hell had I stumbled into?

Bracing my hands on either side of myself, I pushed up until I was sitting. Then, rubbing what felt like a bruise forming on my elbow—another to add to my growing collection—I told the nun standing over me about Margaret's arrival on the shelter's front porch and the man who had pursued her.

I left out nothing. Not my identity or my history with St. Paul's, not the stone, not the explosion, nothing. I would have liked to say it was because I trusted her, but in truth, I was too fucking tired to decide what details to share and what to hold back, and so she got it all.

I sat there, on a dirty, cold stone floor beside a decades-old bucket, and told her about my episode at the hospital, about Sister Ernestine and her arsenal and the burning of the sister house, about finding the shelter in ruins with everyone but Phoenix gone, about the attack on the internet café and the cocoon I'd spun around the man to blame—because, yes, the cocoon had been my doing, my abomination.

I paused at that point to swallow hard and flex the hands that I'd unconsciously curled into fists. Confession might be good for the soul, but it was damned hard when your calling was to help people, not have a direct hand in killing them. And when you still didn't know *how* you'd killed them.

Sister Anne Louise cleared her throat. I hadn't looked at her through any of my monologue and didn't particularly want to now, but I couldn't avoid it forever. I raised my chin, then my gaze, expecting to find horror in hers. Or at least disbelief.

I found neither. Instead, her expression seemed … sad. And resigned. And—evasive?

"You've been through a lot," she said. "I'm sorry for that." She slid the thin sword into its cane casing again and settled the tip of it on the floor. Then, leaning heavily on the polished wood handle, she added, "Things weren't supposed to happen like that."

"Weren't supposed to—" I stared at her, sure I'd misheard, or at least misunderstood. "I'm sorry, was there an alternate way I should have come into possession of a weird, spiderweb-spinning stone that kills people?"

"Actually, yes," said Sister Anne Louise. "But you left the monastery before you could be recruited."

Chapter 24

I had no words. I had no feeling in my butt anymore, either, but that was definitely secondary to the *no words* part. And as I gaped at the nun standing over me, my mouth flapping soundlessly, I was unable to give voice to the single word ricocheting through my brain like an escaped ping pong ball. *Recruited?*

What in the—and wait. She'd known who I was and still made me go through all of that? Maybe I should have cocooned her after all.

"Come," said Sister Anne Louise. "It's best if I show you." She reached a withered hand down to me and, with a strength that probably shouldn't have surprised me by now but still did, pulled me to my feet. Then she turned away and lifted the lantern from its hook.

A muffled *clunk* came from inside the wall, followed by a mechanical scraping and the sound of stone grinding against stone. Slowly, a section of the rough wall rotated to one side, revealing an opening—and beyond that opening, pitch blackness.

Sister Anne Louise looked over her shoulder at me. "Through here," she said, motioning with the lantern as if she expected me to precede her into the void.

As fucking if, I thought, peering into the darkness. Voluntarily step into a black hole in a dank, forgotten cellar at the behest of an ancient nun who, moments before, had threatened to kill me and leave my body down here, never to be found?

I stared at her. "You've got to be kidding."

"I assure you that I'm most serious," Sister Anne

Louise replied. "You want answers? They're that way." She waved the lantern at the void again.

Surreptitiously, I gauged the distance to the cellar stairs and escape. After the last two days, my paranoia was running at an all-time high, and I was inclined to err on the side of caution. On the other hand, Sister Anne Louise was right. I did want answers, especially about the *recruited* part. Scowling, I folded my arms across myself and stood my ground.

"Fine. But you first," I told her.

The old nun chuckled, a dry cackle of sound. "Fair enough," she said, and then stepped through the opening. The dark on the other side was so complete that it almost swallowed her in her entirety, especially given the black of her habit. I could see only her face, floating like an apparition above the lantern's glow when she turned to make sure I followed.

I cast a last glance in the direction of the cellar stairs, but without the lantern's light, they'd disappeared, too. Taking a deep breath, I shuffled after Sister Anne Louise and my answers—I hoped.

"Follow the wall," the nun instructed, forging ahead and taking the light with her, "and keep your head down. The ceiling is—"

I let out a muffled yelp as my skull connected with said ceiling.

"—low," she finished. "Are you all right?"

I lifted the hand not following the wall to a new lump forming on my temple, blinking back tears of pain and irritation.

"Peachy," I snarled, because I was getting tired of feeling like a punching bag. "Damn it, Sister, where are we going?"

"It's not far now," she said by way of an answer that

was no answer at all.

The lantern bobbed in and out of view behind her as she moved away from me again. I held my ground for a moment, seriously considering just turning around. But even if I could have found my way back to the stairs and the monastery above without falling over something and inflicting yet more injury on myself, what then?

I would still have no answers and no idea of where to go from here, and—

"Fuck," I growled into the dark, not caring even a little if I offended my companion. I hunched my head down between my shoulders and groped my way forward in pursuit of the disappearing sister and her light.

The passage—for that's what it had to be, given the roughly fifty feet that I estimated we had shuffled—ended in front of a wooden door. I could tell by the sound of a doorknob twisting and the squeak of hinges as Sister Anne Louise opened it. She reached inside as I arrived beside her, and an electric light flared to life on the other side.

I blinked a few times in its glare. Then, as my eyes adjusted and I saw the interior beyond, my jaw went slack. I gaped at the room, then at Sister Anne Louise, then at the room again. No dank, dark cellar, this. It was more like … an office? It wasn't large. I guessed it to be roughly eight feet by ten feet, but it was hard to tell with the sheer amount of stuff crammed into it. My gaze slid over the contents, and my first impression corrected itself. Not stuff. Papers. Papers and books and files and rolls of more papers were stacked on every available surface—the floor, all the shelves lining the room, a table in the center …

And the edge of every step of a narrow, circular staircase in the back corner that snaked upward and ended in a closed trap door.

"My bedroom," said Sister Anne Louise at my elbow,

pointing at the trap door. "I'm in charge of the archive." Her point became an encompassing wave that took in the room.

Archive? I looked sideways at her. "I didn't even know the monastery *had* an archive," I said, and then I raised an eyebrow. "Wait. Mother Annunciata allowed someone other than her to maintain it?"

"It's not the monastery archive. It belongs to The Obsidian Sisterhood, and Mother Annunciata knows nothing about us." Sister Anne Louise pursed her lips thoughtfully, making them even more wrinkly, and added, "At least, I didn't think she did."

"The Obsidian Sis—" I broke off as my brain belatedly added two and two together. "You said I left the monastery before I could be recruited. Into that?"

"Into that," the nun agreed. "The Obsidian Sisterhood is older than the church itself, formed to keep that"—she pointed toward my pocket in which the stone was tucked— "and the others like it safe."

My gaze followed her pointing finger, and I stared down at my jeans, processing her words. Older than the church … others like it …

I opened my mouth to ask a question, then staggered, falling against Sister Anne Louise as the stone in my pocket abruptly gained what felt like a hundred pounds, throwing me off balance. In the same instant, a commotion erupted above us, distant and muffled but still identifiable as voices —male ones—raised in anger, along with what sounded like the crash of furniture being thrown around.

My heart dived earthward, and all thoughts evaporated except one. They'd found me.

Again.

CHAPTER 25

"SWEET FANCY MOSES IN A MUFFIN TIN," GROWLED SISTER Anne Louise as her claw-like fingers set me upright and away from her. "You were followed."

I opened my mouth to tell her that I'd been careful, that it had taken me an hour longer to make the drive than it should have, because I'd watched my rearview mirror obsessively, taken an exit off the 401 any time I flagged a car as suspicious, driven random routes through the smaller centers along the way because it was easier to pick out vehicles there than it was on the highway …

But explanation was pointless. The footsteps that thudded over our heads made it clear that I hadn't been as careful as I'd thought. Somehow, they had followed me in spite of my precautions, and now they'd found me, and—

I dug my fingernails into my palms, fighting back the onset of panic and the desire to take the stone from my pocket. I really, really didn't want to go that route again, I told myself. Really. Not when I still hadn't recovered from the last time and didn't know what it—or I—might do this time.

Sister Anne Louise had hustled her habit across the room to the table and set the lantern down, and now she was flinging papers helter-skelter and muttering under her breath. I took a deep breath and dug my fingernails in harder, trying to slow my heartbeat and make myself think. It was impossible.

Between exhaustion and injury and emotional trauma, my reserves were too low. Dangerously low. The edges of reason had begun to fray, and all I could think about was how all of the women who lived and prayed here, all of the women I'd once called sisters, would die as the nuns of the St. Mary's sister house had died … and the women of the Mary Magdalene. And how I would be alone again, thrust back to square one, with no answers and no idea of—

Sister Anne Louise shoved something against my chest and held it there. "Well?" she barked, "take it!"

I stared down at the thick, leather-bound book and the arthritis-twisted fingers pressing it against me, but I made no move to hold it. A book? She was giving me a book?

The old nun huffed impatiently. She grabbed one of my hands, lifted it, and slapped it across the book. Above us, something heavy scraped across the floor of Sister Anne Louise's bedroom—the bed, perhaps, or the desk. A nun didn't have much furniture in her room—not at St. Paul's, anyway.

Sister Anne Louise's lips thinned to non-existent. She grabbed my chin in her hand and glared at me. "Listen to me. I've been working on this"—she tapped the book's cover with a finger of her other hand—"since Sister Margaret left. It's a summary of sorts. You won't find all your answers, but you might find enough to get you started. Now, you need to go before they find the trap door."

Backpedaling under the pressure of the nun's hand against the book she'd given me, I glanced at the spiral stairs and the square outline in the ceiling above them. If they were moving furniture, they were already looking for the trap door, and if they were already looking …

"They didn't follow me," I whispered.

"What?" Sister Anne Louise paused in her pushing, and I wobbled for an instant, then caught my balance.

"They didn't follow me," I repeated. "They knew

where to find your room, and they know about the trap door. They're looking for—"

A triumphant shout from the room above cut me off. They weren't just looking for the trap door anymore, they'd found it. For a moment, neither Sister Anne Louise nor I moved—or breathed. Then she shoved me toward the door again, hard.

"Go!" she hissed. "Go now—no, wait! You'll need the lantern."

The old nun darted back to the table, grabbed the lantern, and then seized my arm and propelled me into the passage. I shuffled the journal to one arm and caught the lantern with my free hand as she thrust it at me.

"Wait," I cried as she began shutting the door. "What about you?"

Watery, pale blue eyes met mine for an instant, a world of knowing and sadness in their depths. "The trap door is locked from this side," she said calmly, "but it won't hold for long. I'll buy you as much time as I can, but you need to move fast. You need to get away. Do you understand?"

I shook my head, too. In denial, in despair, in grief for what I sensed coming.

"No," I whispered. "No, I don't understand, Sister. I don't understand any of this."

"I know," she said. "And I wish we had more time, but we don't. Now, run, Sister Monica. Run as if the fate of the entire world rested on you, because I think it might."

And with that, she stepped back and before I could stop her, slammed the door closed on me. The lantern flame guttered in the gust of wind, then steadied again. My heartbeat did not. For a moment, shock and indecision held me immobile, and then voices that had been upstairs a moment before were suddenly in the room with Sister

Anne Louise, galvanizing me into action—but not in the direction the nun had told me to go.

Instead, I threw my entire weight at the door—once, twice, a third time—still clutching the journal in one hand and the lantern in the other. The latter swung wildly, spilling tiny rivers of flaming oil onto the floor at my feet and the wood of the door. I didn't care. I knew only that I couldn't—wouldn't—lose another woman because of this godforsaken stone that I carried. I readied myself for a fourth assault, this time bracing to deliver a kick that would carry all the power of three martial arts and two black belts behind—

A flash of purple briefly illuminated the edges of the door, and a scream erupted in the room beyond. An old woman's scream, high-pitched and thready … and then abruptly cut off.

My foot dropped like cement to the floor, and I staggered into stillness. I was too late.

I stared at the flames licking their way up the wooden door. That Sister Anne Louise had known she would die, I had no doubt. That I hadn't stood a chance of saving her, I was equally certain. Neither of those eased the loss.

But standing here waiting for them to come for me next wouldn't ease it, either.

"Run," Sister Anne Louise's memory whispered. *"Run as if the fate of the entire world rested on you, Sister Monica, because I think it might."*

"Run," echoed Sister Ernestine. *"They can never get it, do you understand? You have to keep it away from them."*

Something thudded against the other side of the door. They'd be through soon, and if I was still here, Sister Anne Louise would have sacrificed herself for nothing. I would not let that happen. I whirled and, holding the journal to my chest and the lantern high, did as I'd been bidden once again.

I ran.

After what seemed like a century later but was only a moment or two, I stumbled out of the passage and into the cellar, my chest heaving with fury and frustration and pent-up grief. Yet another woman had fallen to whoever it was that wanted this blasted stone, and I still had nothing. No answers, no direction, no idea of what I faced or what I was supposed to do.

Let alone how I would do it.

The sound of wood splintering came from the other end of the passage I'd just left. Voices followed. Male, angry, not English, and approaching fast. Whatever Sister Anne Louise had done to secure the door when she'd closed it had given way, and they'd broken through into the tunnel. They had no light of their own, but they could doubtless see mine.

A fresh surge of adrenaline shot through me, and I gauged the distance to the rickety stairs. Dear sweet Mary, I wouldn't make it—and the voices were getting nearer.

Hail Mary Magdalene, full of grace, come to my aid …

I held the lantern high as I scanned the dank, dark space, searching for something to fight with, somewhere to hide, something to—

My gaze landed on the hook by the passage opening. The one that Sister Anne Louise had taken the lantern from, triggering the door.

Excitement marked the voices, now. They were halfway through the passage.

"Run!" said sisters Anne Louise and Ernestine together.

In two strides, I was beneath the hook. I turned to face the cellar stairs and locked their position into my mind's eye, took a quick breath, and without moving my feet so much as an inch, twisted around to hang the lantern on the hook. Then I opened its little glass side door and blew out the flame, plunging the cellar back into darkness.

The voices in the passage escalated in volume and tone, and one gave a shout of pain as the low ceiling took its toll. I'd done it. I'd eradicated what little guiding light my pursuers might have had. But that hadn't been my only goal, and it wasn't enough, and nothing else was happening, and *fucking hell*.

My stomach dropped into my toes. Had I made a mistake? If I'd been wrong, if I'd extinguished my only light for no reason—

A muffled clunk sounded inside the wall, followed by the same mechanical grinding I'd heard before. I slapped a hand over my mouth to stifle a shout of triumph, shoring up knees that wanted to sag in relief. No sound of stone grating on stone had ever been more beautiful.

But I had no time to listen to it, because if the owners of the voices didn't get through the passage before it closed, they'd look for another way. For that matter, there might others who were already searching. I had to get out of the monastery before they found me.

Aiming myself in the direction of where I pictured the stairs to be, I groped and staggered toward escape, tripping over bits of debris and swallowing a giggle born of sheer stress when I kicked the abandoned bucket yet again.

That damned bucket.

In the end, finding the stairs was more a matter of falling into them and scraping both shins than of skilled navigation, but I didn't pause. I didn't dare. Still clutching the book Sister Anne Louise had given me, I stumbled upward, careful to keep against the wall. Breaking an ankle now—or even spraining one—would be tantamount to death.

I reached the door at the top, found the knob and twisted it, and promptly sprawled face first into the corridor beyond when someone in the hallway pulled just as I pushed. I landed with the journal squarely against my solar plexus, and every last ounce of air left my body and refused to return. For precious moments, I didn't move except to blink back tears of pain and panic as I willed the spasm in my diaphragm to ease. Then, just as it did, the hem of a black habit came into view.

A nun.

My breath left me again, and my heart skipped an entire series of beats as relief tangled with panic and tried not to become despair. *Not Annunciata,* I thought, *please don't be Mother Annuncia*—

Firm, gentle hands grasped my arms and lifted me to my feet. "This way," a voice urged. "There's a door into the back garden."

I allowed myself to be pushed along the corridor and steered around corner after corner as I tried to get my bearings. I remembered the garden, but I also recalled that there was a six-foot-high stone wall around it, complete with a locked gate and—

We'd reached the exterior door, and warm fingers pressed a key into the palm of my hand. "Lock the gate behind you," my benefactor said, "and throw the key as far into the woods as you can. I hid the spare. It will take them a while to find it."

Remembering the destruction my pursuers had wrought in Toronto—if they were one and the same—I doubted they would need a key, but I kept the thought to myself as the nun pushed me through the door and onto a small, flagstone terrace on the other side. My gratitude, however, needed to be spoken.

"Wait," I said, transferring the key to my book-holding

hand and catching the edge of the door before it closed. "I don't know who you are, but—"

A thunderous boom cut me off, rumbling through the ground beneath our feet. The nun and I both flinched and ducked as the entire building trembled, shaking loose a century's worth of dust from between the limestone blocks. As the echoes died away, I stared past the nun's black-clad shoulder at the flickering light fixture hanging by its wires beside a massive, jagged hole in the ceiling. Its light was faint, but it was enough to illuminate the rubble below it through the dust.

Horror paralyzed me. It was happening again, just like the sister house and the shelter, and the impulse, the need, to go to the aid of the sisters inside clawed at me. But so did the words of sisters Anne Louise and Ernestine—and the sacrifices they'd made to get me this far.

A soft hand covered mine where I'd wrapped my fingers around the doorframe. I tore my gaze from the billows of dust and fallen timbers and met the calm, utterly certain gray eyes of my rescuer.

"You cannot help them," she said. "You must go."

"I can't just leave," I whispered. "I can't."

"They knew the risks when they joined the Obsidian Sisterhood," she said, prying my fingers loose. "We all did. We protect the stones. They do not protect us. Now run."

Before I could react, another explosion shook the building, and she thrust my hand away and slammed the door—yet another one—in my face. Sheer reflex drove me to throw myself at it and grab for the knob, but I was too late. Through the rumble of whatever was falling apart inside came the distinct click of the deadbolt and the end of my internal debate. The nun had made my decision for me—and handed me a brand-new question in the process.

Just how big was this Obsidian Sisterhood, anyway?

Chapter 26

In the few minutes it took to reach the back of the garden, adrenaline, shock, and my questions about the Obsidian Sisterhood had given way to severe irritation.

As I locked the gate behind me and hurled the key into the woods with all the strength of my pent-up frustration, I decided I was getting seriously tired of this shit. Tired of running, tired of things blowing up, tired of hurting, tired of not having a clue why any of it was happening in the first place, and tired—*fucking* tired—of people dying.

I sniffled inelegantly and swiped my sleeve across my cheeks and then under my nose, noting as I did the streaks of dirt on the garment. And the cobwebs clinging to my elbow. Real cobwebs.

Not that the ones in the stone weren't real when they wrapped around and through my hand. I was fucking tired of those, too.

And tired, period. And fucking tired of being tired, and—

And just *fuck*.

I swayed on my feet, trembling with delayed shock as I surveyed my surroundings and tried to get my bearings. I hadn't been in these woods in more than twenty years, and any path I might have trod back then had long since grown over. Nothing looked familiar. I couldn't remember how far the nearest road was, or in what direction it lay, and dear sweet Mary, even if I found my way out of here, I still had to find my way back to where I'd parked the damned car, and—

Locking my knees against their desire to fold under me,

I put the brakes on my hysteria and inhaled a slow, deep breath through my nostrils, held it, then exhaled it just as slowly through parted lips. Panic would get me nowhere, I told myself. I could do this. Mostly because I had no choice, but … whatever. The point was, I *would* get out of here, and then—

I looked down at the journal I held against my chest, my arms folded across it and my knuckles pale with the ferocity of their grip.

And then I would hope to hell that I would find the answers I so desperately needed in whatever this was that Sister Anne Louise had shoved at me.

I flinched at the sound of another explosion in the monastery. Sweet Mary, what was with these people and blowing things up? Glancing over my shoulder, I saw flames erupt from the windows and roof, and I faltered as responsibility for the nuns trapped inside tugged at me. Then, deliberately, I hardened myself against the unfolding tragedy. I could do nothing for them, and I owed it to the women—all of them—who'd put themselves in the way of harm to protect me so that I could protect the stone.

All of them *so far*, because the body count was still climbing.

Grimly, I surveyed the burning edifice, disregarding the flames and focusing on orienting myself. From somewhere in the distance came what sounded like the steady beat of a drum—or maybe footsteps marching. The sound held no meaning or memory for me, so I filtered it out in favor of another that was nearer and coming from my right—sirens wailing their approach, which meant streets, which meant …

I closed my eyes, forcing my mind back ten years, then twenty, then thirty, into the heart of the time when I had called the monastery my home, and the sisters had been my family.

Well, most of them, anyway.

I shut out the sirens and the roar of flames devouring the roof. I pushed harder at my mind. I remembered my room at the front of the building, and how I'd loved the way the morning sun streamed in, because—

"East," I muttered to myself. "I faced east."

Another detail surfaced. I'd always thought that the "back" garden—the one I'd come through just now—had been inaccurately named, because it sat to the south rather than the actual rear of the building. Suddenly, the orientation I'd been striving for settled over me like a warm, familiar blanket, and my eyes snapped open.

I knew where I was. Knew that I stood beside the monastery right now, not behind it, and that if I made a quarter turn to my right, I'd be facing east again, the direction I'd—

Two black-clad figures burst through the back door into the garden, clinging to one another as they stumbled away from the structure, one of them sobbing. Responsibility tugged again, but even if I'd wanted to go to the nuns, I had no way of getting back into the garden because I'd tossed the key away, and—

As if she'd felt my eyes on her, the nun who wasn't weeping turned toward me—but she wasn't just a nun. She was Annunciata. She was the Mother Superior, and that was hatred glittering in the gaze locked on mine. Hatred, and fear, and—

A garden and a universe away, Annunciata opened her mouth and screeched over the roar and crackle of flames, "She's here! The woman you want is here!"

Running, I thought as I turned tail and bolted through the trees, had apparently become my new way of life.

I'M PRETTY SURE I STARTLED THE LIVING DAYLIGHTS OUT OF the firefighter I almost ran over as I barreled out of the woods at the side of the monastery and bolted across the lawn. I didn't pause to check on him—or her—just as I hadn't waited to see who might answer Annunciata's summons. My entire focus was on not tripping over anything that would send me sprawling and end my head-long flight.

Well, that and the drumming sound that had followed me, getting persistently closer. At one point, whether it was because of reverberations from the trees or the stone building I paralleled, the sound seemed to be converging on me from all directions, but I hadn't stopped to check on that, either. If anything, I'd run faster—and regretted with every jarring stride that I hadn't taken up long-distance running in my older age.

I sprinted down the driveway, my chest burning and breath coming in gasps as I leaped over hoses. I dodged an outstretched hand here and a concerned, helmet-framed face there, my whole focus on the open gates at the end. Firefighters, police, and paramedics were all on site by now. Perhaps their presence would give pause to any pursuers. Perhaps it would not, and they, too, would be in danger because of my very presence.

I didn't want to find out which.

I was almost at the end. The wrought-iron gates had been thrown wide to let in the emergency vehicles, and a police car was parked across the opening to prevent gawkers from entering the grounds. The front end of the vehicle nudged up against the gate post, but there was room to get around the back end. Or there would have been, if it weren't for the burly, much-younger-than-me cop standing there, wide-legged and braced to grab me when I tried.

I didn't miss a beat.

I veered right, tore my left hand from the journal, and used it to vault myself over the car's hood. The heat from the idling engine burned my palm, distracting me for a split second so that I stumbled on my landing, but I recovered my footing and plunged through the onlookers onto the street. The grinning garden gnome was gone from the lawn across the road. How weird. And weird, too, what details the mind noted under duress.

I swerved again. Now I was clear of the crowd and running toward the vehicle I'd parked beneath a towering oak tree in front of a neighboring house.

I'd almost made it when I saw them. Or rather, heard them.

"Sister Monica! Sister! Over here!" a woman's familiar voice yelled in between intermittent but insistent honks from a car horn—and over the drumming that was beginning to fade into the distance.

"Sister Monica!"

My steps hesitated, then slowed. I stopped in the middle of the street and cast a glance back at the onlookers, searching for the owner of the voice, but I saw no one I knew, and no one looking my way. The crowd was far more focused on the blazing monastery than on the dirt-smeared, wild-eyed old woman who'd elbowed her way through them. Except for the cop, whose head bobbed up and down as he tried to see over the crowd. I had about thirty seconds before he spotted me.

The drums were almost gone.

"Sister Monica!" A hand seized my wrist, and I spun around to stare slack-jawed at—

"*Phoenix?*"

My brain struggled to reconcile what my eyes told it they saw, but it felt like someone had poured sludge into my brain synapses. It was no wonder I hadn't recognized her voice, because the context was all wrong, and her being here in Kingston was all wrong, and—I shook my head, partly in denial but mostly in an attempt to clear it.

"You can't be here," I blurted, panting. "You're in Toronto."

"Except I'm obviously not." Phoenix tugged at my arm. "I'll explain everything in the car, I promise, but we have to go. *Now.*"

The car? I looked over my shoulder at Dawson's vehicle, but Phoenix was towing me away from that and toward a four-door gray sedan pulled over on the opposite side of the street. My sense of befuddlement increased. Phoenix, here in Kingston. A car that wasn't the one I'd arrived in, and—

The sedan's front passenger door swung open, and a woman leaned across from the driver's seat, as impossibly familiar as Phoenix. "Get in," Detective Dawson barked. "They're right behind you!"

They? As in more than just the cop at the gate? I squelched the impulse to do a shoulder-check to see for myself as Phoenix shoved me toward the open door. I ducked in time to avoid cold-cocking myself on the frame and sprawled awkwardly across the passenger seat beside Dawson.

The door slammed behind me, the rear one opened and closed, and Phoenix yelled, "Go!"

Without hesitation, Dawson gunned it. We shot away from the curb with a squeal of tires, and I grabbed for the armrest to pull myself upright. I opened my mouth to tell Dawson that I hoped to hell this wasn't the work vehicle she'd spoken of—because that would *so* not be good—but a new voice from the back seat stopped me.

"Seatbelt, Sister Monica," said the voice. "We can't afford more injury to you." Female again, but not famil—

I froze, staring straight ahead as icy prickles ran down my spine. Wait. I *did* know that voice, but—no, I couldn't, because it wasn't just out of context, it was impossible. Because …

My head whipped around. I stared into the backseat and the expressionless brown eyes of the woman I'd traced to the monastery. The woman who had died—or so I'd thought—on the front porch of the Mary Magdalene House for Women.

"Sister Margaret?" I croaked.

My few remaining brain cells fused together.

CHAPTER 27

"You're sure you'll be okay?" I asked Phoenix. "I don't like leaving you on your own like this."

Phoenix raised an eyebrow and looked over one shoulder, then the other at the shabby motel room behind her. She shrugged. "I agree that the place is sketchy," she said, "but it's not *that* sketchy. I'll keep the door locked, and I think I can handle a cockroach or two. Besides, I have this to keep me entertained, remember? I'll be fine."

She nodded down at the journal she'd confiscated from me in the vehicle—*confiscated* being a mild term for the way she'd pounced on it when she'd learned it had come from the monastery and Sister Anne Louise.

"Did it belong to the Obsidian Sisterhood?" she'd demanded, leaning forward to peer between the front seats at it, her eyes wide. "It did, didn't it?"

"You know about—" I'd broken off as Phoenix undid her seatbelt and lunged between me and Dawson to snatch the journal from my lap.

"Seatbelt," Dawson had ordered tersely, and the young woman had flopped back into her own seat.

"Yeah, yeah," she said. "But *Obsidian Sisterhood.*"

I'd twisted in my seat to look at her, but my gaze hadn't made it past the skeletal nun beside her whose presence I hadn't yet wrapped my head around. A skeletal nun whose hair was no longer matted, who didn't stink, who no longer wore rags, and who was undeniably not dead. But …

I'd subsided back into the passenger seat and looked over at Dawson. "How?" I'd mumbled through lips that felt as numb with disbelief as the rest of me.

"Long story," Dawson had said. "We'll get you caught up, I promise. But first, we need to get you clear of the area. We have a motel room at the edge of town. We can hole up there for the night. Make a plan for what's next. You good with that?"

I had no idea if the idea was sound, but I liked that someone else had come up with it and all I had to do was agree. So I nodded my head, Dawson nodded hers, and now, forty-five minutes of evasive driving maneuvers later, I was clutching a room key and dithering over Phoenix remaining on her own.

Which was highly annoying, because damn it, I didn't dither.

"I'll be fine," Phoenix said again, steering me one-handed out the door and onto the veranda that ran across the front of the motel's second floor. "I've already heard most of what Sister Margaret has to tell you, and I'd much rather stay here and read the book." She nodded her head toward the journal she'd dropped on one of the beds, then continued, "Seriously, Sister Monica, the restaurant is right across the street. If anything happens—which it won't—I promise you'll hear me yelling. Now go eat, listen to Sister Margaret, and figure out what you want to do next—especially about the Mages. Oh, and don't forget to bring me a cheeseburger when you come back. With fries. And a chocolate shake."

She gave me a final push as I tried to turn back to her —because *mages?*—and the door closed on me. It popped open again before I could blink.

"Wait," she said, "make that a strawberry shake. And one of those fruit pie thingies."

The door closed again—then opened just enough for me to hear her hastily added, "Never mind! Make it chocolate. For sure chocolate. Please and thank you!" before it stayed shut.

I stared at the rust-pocked number 213 for a moment, then sighed and pocketed the key. Turning away, I plodded down the metal stairs to where Dawson and the not-dead nun waited for me.

"I still don't like leaving her alone," I muttered.

Arms crossed as she leaned against a pillar supporting the motel veranda above us, Dawson raised an eyebrow and sent a pointed look at the fast-food restaurant which sat, as Phoenix had pointed out, on the other side of the street.

"Fifty feet, tops." she said. "That's how far away we'll be. I can hit something a lot smaller than a man at that distance, believe me."

I raised my own eyebrow. "You have your …?"

She held her blazer slightly aside, revealing her sidearm. "No way was I leaving it behind under the circumstances."

"Is that—" I stopped, because questioning a cop on the legality of carrying a gun seemed … what? Presumptuous? Impertinent? Both?

Dawson didn't seem to feel the same way about my question. "Legal?" she finished. "That depends."

"On?"

"Whether or not I use it. Now, I don't know about you, but I'm starving, and Sister Margaret looks like she's going to fall over if she doesn't sit down soon."

My stomach gave an uneasy roll at the very mention of food, and I sent a baleful look at the nun who leaned against Dawson's sedan on the other side of the parking lot. I didn't give two figs what Sister Margaret thought, because I was supposed to trust the woman who'd tossed me a stone that held unimaginable dark powers and then disappeared from my life? I didn't think so.

As if she'd heard my thoughts, Sister Margaret stood away from the car and walked over to join us. "I know you're angry with me," she said, "and you have every right. But I have much to explain, and we don't have a lot of time. *You* don't have a lot of time."

Her choice of words didn't help her cause. I scowled at her, then at Dawson.

"Explain to me why I'm supposed to listen to the dead nun?"

Dawson's lips twitched, but she straightened them again. "Because she's *not* dead," she said, "and as soon as she heard about the shelter and St. Mary's, she turned herself in, because she was worried about you."

"Not convinced," I said.

Dawson sighed, straightened up from her leaning post, and crossed her arms.

"Look," she said, "Sister Margaret hasn't told me much about what's going on beyond this secret sisterhood thing, but if she can refuse medical treatment, convince me to take an emergency leave of absence to come and rescue you, and insist on accompanying me on that rescue, then *you*"—she uncrossed her arms to jab a finger into my chest —"can give her fifteen minutes of your time. All right? Now, can we please go eat?"

"You know what?" I growled. "I have a better idea."

Digging my fingers into my pocket, I extracted the stone and flung it at the nun's chest. "There," I said, pulling my hand back in a *done* kind of way. "You can have it ba—"

But before I could finish, the stone ricocheted off Sister Margaret and slammed into my open palm with enough force to spin me around and almost knock me from my feet. I staggered, caught my balance, and stared slack-jawed at the shining threads that still wound around and through my hand—and now extended up my arm and disappeared beneath my sleeve, as well. A cold knot of foreboding unfurled in the pit of my belly.

"The fuck …" I whispered. I looked over my shoulder at the skeletal but clean nun standing beside a grim-jawed Dawson.

"I'm afraid," Sister Margaret said quietly, "that it's not that simple."

THE THREE OF US WALKED ACROSS THE STREET IN SILENCE as the sun dropped behind the trees to the left of the little enclave of buildings that included the motel, the restaurant, a gas station, and—rather bizarrely, I thought—a carpet wholesaler. Once inside the fast-food place, we ordered at the counter—Dawson insisted that I eat, despite my protest that the knot in my belly left no room for food—and then the detective carried her tray to a table near the door where she could watch for potential trouble. I chose a window seat a few tables away, where I had a clear view of the door to room 213 across the street.

I waited until the skeletal Sister Margaret was seated, then, without further ado, gave voice to the question that had been on the tip of my tongue since the stone had boomeranged back to me in the motel parking lot.

"What the actual *fuck* is going on?" I snarled across the burgers, fries, and paper cups of coffee between us—none of which I was likely to consume. When Margaret didn't answer in the point zero two seconds I allotted for her response, I demanded, "Well?"

And then, when she did open her mouth to respond, I waved her silent, because I wasn't done yet. Hell, with what I'd been through in the past two days, I hadn't even started.

"Do you have any idea what you've put me through?" I asked. "What you've done? I've lost everything, damn it. *Everything.*" I held up both my hands and ticked off my losses on my fingers as I continued. "The sister house, the shelter, my life's work, my home, my friends, the women I was supposed to protect—"

"This isn't about you, Sister Monica."

Sister Margaret's interruption was a bare murmur, but her words stopped my tirade in its tracks, much the same as a fist to my gut would have done. And they made the air hiss from me the way a fist would have, too.

Because holy *oof*—she was right. When had I become so wrapped up in myself that I'd forgotten the very nature of my calling? My vow to serve others, to put them before myself and do everything in my power to care for them? A vow made not in a vainglorious attempt to garner praise, but in a heartfelt, soul-deep certainty that it was simply the right thing to do? What I was supposed to do. What I had been born to do.

"Shit," I whispered, grateful as always that "clean" language was not a part of the same calling. I braced an elbow on the table beside my untouched coffee and placed my fist against my mouth, letting the full impact of my self-ishness sink in.

And then ... then I took a long, deep breath and let it go again, because if there was one thing I'd learned in my sixty-nine years—in spite of the teachings of my church—it was that guilt solved nothing. No matter how hard I worked at my calling, I was just as human as the next person and just as worthy of giving myself grace. It was a lesson I had always tried to impart to the shelter residents: When you made mistakes, you apologized and then moved on as best you could, because that was all that you could do. It was all any of us could do.

Well, that and do better the next time.

I looked out the window to check that room 213 remained intact, then met Sister Margaret's gaze across the table. "I'm sorry," I said.

"As am I," she said, sighing. "Because you're right, you *have* lost a lot, and you were thrown into this completely unprepared, and I wish it could have been different."

Sister Anne Louise had said much the same.

"But it can't?" I hazarded.

"No. It can't."

My gut tightened. I was right. I wouldn't be eating my burger.

"You'd better start at the beginning," I said.

Sister Margaret gave a short, mirthless chuckle. "If I start at the beginning, we'll be here for days," she said. "How much was Sister Anne Louise able to tell you?"

"Not a lot. She told me that the Obsidian Sisterhood was formed to keep the stone—sorry, the *stones* plural—safe, but that was about it. We'd just gotten to the archive when we heard them in her room above."

"They followed you," Margaret murmured. "I was afraid they would. They're getting better at tracking us—I just wish I knew how."

Speaking of following … my entire body tensed as the bell above the door gave a merry little jangle. Two men entered, one barely visible behind the other from where I sat, and my gaze flicked to Dawson, seeking her reaction.

"Problem?" Sister Margaret murmured, watching me.

Seeming oblivious to my attention on her, Dawson sipped her coffee, then smiled and lifted one hand to wiggle her fingers in the kind of little wave one gave a—

I looked back at the men as they separated, and a curly-haired toddler peeked at me over the shoulder of the shorter one. The breath returned to my lungs. I shook my head.

"No," I answered Sister Margaret. "No problem." I left out the *not this time* part and returned to the *being followed* issue.

"Actually, I don't think they did track me," I said. I told her about Mother Annunciata's hostile reception, her attempted attack on me, and then her shrieked, *"She's here! The woman you want is here!"* when she saw me outside the garden wall.

Margaret's mouth stretched thin. "I wish I could say I was surprised," she said, "but I'm not. I've always wondered whether Annunciata might have been placed at St. Paul's because they suspected some of us were of the Obsidian Sisterhood."

"You keep saying they." I was tiring of the mystery— and the ambiguity. "Who in heaven's name *are* they?"

She snorted. "Hardly of heaven, believe me. And *they* are of the church and government and every organization in the entire world that seeks power, Sister Monica. They are the leaders. The ones who create the laws that raise them up at the expense of others. Who have tried, time and again, to take away the very essence of humanity because they would rather rule through fear than love."

She took a deep breath. "And if they get the stones, I think they'll destroy us all—including themselves."

CHAPTER 28

Fifteen minutes, Dawson had said. *"Give her fifteen minutes of your time."*

And that was all it had taken to turn the remainder of my world on its head. Because a secret sisterhood had been bad enough, but one that was several millennia old? That had been formed to hide an alien being that had landed on Earth with six stones of immeasurable power in his—her—its possession?

My brain boggled and then boggled again, but not over the pronoun issue. My stupefaction was more about the idea that thousands of women over thousands of years had quietly, fiercely, and steadfastly kept something as enormous—figuratively speaking—as the stones out of the hands of those who would have used—would still use— their power, no matter the cost.

And it was also about the idea that all their efforts might have been in vain, because now—now, after those same thousands of years—the alien and his stones had disappeared. Poof. Gone.

Well, except for the one currently tucked into my front jeans pocket that refused to leave, of course. But I digressed, because the stones' disappearance was one thing. Their disappearance from six different locations—seven, if you counted the alien's departure as well—around the globe was quite another.

And the boggling mind was about the alien thing, too, because *alien*? What the fuck was I supposed to do with that?

I rested my elbows on the table and raked my fingers

through my short hair, then rubbed them down my face, then let them fall into my lap. I pulled my gaze from the motel I'd been staring at through the window—absently noting as I did that the streetlights had come on along the road between me and it—and looked across at Sister Margaret.

"Again," I told her. "Start with the alien, and tell me again." And sweet holy Mary, let some of it make sense this time.

"His name is Methuselah," she said.

There went another brain cell. I stared at her, half hoping she was kidding, knowing she was not.

"Methuselah," I repeated. "You named him—them—it—Methuselah."

"Eventually, yes. He was probably called something else in the beginning—he likely had many names—but Methuselah is the one that stuck."

That would certainly explain—and put a whole new spin on—the world's oldest man story, but that was another digression.

I opened my mouth to tell her I didn't care what he was called, decided that perhaps I didn't have the patience for a repeat of the story after all, and waved away my own words along with hers.

"Let's just skip ahead to what happened eight months ago," I muttered, putting one elbow back on the table and pinching the bridge of my nose in an effort to hold back the headache forming between my eyebrows.

"Yes," Margaret agreed. "Let's. I'm sure Phoenix can catch you up on details from the journal later. I like her, by the way. She's smart."

"I like her, too, which is why I keep trying to remove her from this mess." My tone held a deliberate note of warning, and Sister Margaret inclined her head in acknowledgment.

"Of course."

"Eight months ago," I reminded her.

"The first news came from our sister house in Seoul," she said. "We were late getting it, because Mother Annunciata doesn't allow phone calls, of course. We've had to rely on coded messages inside personal letters from another sister house for all our news, so we didn't know about the Seoul stone until it had been missing for a week already. Our contact sister house let us know over the next few weeks about the other stones disappearing as well. Then, just over six months ago, the last stone was taken, and a day later, Methuselah disappeared, too. That's when things became critical."

I took a moment to unpack what she'd said, starting with the easiest point. "Seoul?"

"The Obsidian Sisterhood spans every border and every faith. The sister house in South Korea has guarded their stone since before the first Mongol invasion."

"The Mongols ... "

"Were also after the stones, yes."

"Sweet Mary," I muttered. "How far back does the sisterhood go?"

"How long have women been persecuted?" Margaret asked in response.

Given that my entire education had taken place within a church-run school many decades before, my recollection of history was murky at best. "The Spanish Inquisition?" I hazarded.

She laughed a short laugh. "Think further back than that, Sister Monica. Much, much further. Before the Inquisition came hunts that were spread over centuries, and before those, the laws, and before those, the stripping of our rights and the restrictions on our roles in society."

I frowned past my nose-pinch. "That sounds like you're talking about the patriarchy itself," I said. "But that dates back to …" I trailed off at the grimness of her expression.

"The beginnings of agricultural society, according to some theories," Margaret agreed with my unfinished sentence, "but more likely Sumerian times, when people were needed to produce more to support the elites, and women became the commodity needed to produce those people. And yes, we've been hiding the stones for that long."

I wondered how many brain cells could boggle before I had none left. The sheer magnitude of the timeline the nun suggested, the scope of the interest in the stones, the—

The bell above the door jangled again, cutting my thoughts short. Three men entered this time, all dressed in jeans and t-shirts and wearing sunglasses, reminding me of my first assailant outside the shelter. They paused just inside the door, appearing to scan the tables, and the skin over my entire body went tight as adrenaline surged through my veins, readying me for fight or flight—or both.

I glanced at Dawson, my touchstone. This time, the detective, too, looked poised for trouble, and my heart rate kicked up another notch. As if she sensed my tension, Dawson lifted her hand from the table, palm turned slightly toward me in a *wait* gesture, and a second later, on the far side of the restaurant, a woman sitting alone waved her hand in the air. The three men smiled and waved back, then threaded their way toward her.

The rush of adrenaline subsided, leaving shakiness in its wake and a faint ripple of panic around my edges. I checked again on room 213—it was still there, its brass number illuminated now by the light above the door—and then, ignoring Sister Margaret's sharp look, I closed my eyes. I was no good to anyone, least of all myself, if I let fear get the upper hand. I knew that. And after all the fights I'd been in during my years of protecting the women of the shelter, I knew better.

Focusing on the rise and fall of my chest and belly, I reached for the stillness at my core, the place where clarity and calm existed even when a storm raged around me. I'd used the meditation technique countless times. It was how I centered myself. How I'd learned to shut out the noise and connect with that which was greater—greater than the storm, greater than me.

But for the first time in I couldn't remember how long, I couldn't reach it. The stillness was there, but it was ephemeral at best—too hazy to grasp. As soon as I touched it, it moved tantalizingly out of reach, adding to my frustration.

And to the damned ripple of panic.

I forced my eyes open again. Sister Margaret was still watching me with concern.

"Are you okay?" she asked.

"No," I said. "No, I am not."

"I know this is a lot to take in," she said, "but—"

Caught off guard and still recovering from my adrenaline crash, I burst out laughing—the kind of harsh, unfunny laughter that drew the attention of half the patrons in the restaurant and made Dawson, seven tables away, give a slight shake of her head. *Tone it down*, the gesture said. *You're drawing too much attention.*

Or maybe it was, *Fuck, woman, you've really lost it, haven't you?*

She had no idea.

Either way, I clamped my teeth and lips shut, dug my fingernails into my legs through my jeans, and brought myself back under control. Because yes, it was a lot to take in, but the sun hadn't even set yet, and I suspected Margaret and I had still barely scratched the surface, and poor Phoenix was still at the motel, waiting for her food. We needed to wrap this up. *I* needed to wrap this up.

"You said things became critical when Methuselah went missing," I reminded Margaret. Why?"

"You've seen what the stone I gave you can do."

She wasn't talking about the boomerang effect. The spiderwebs through and around my wrist pulled taut as memories of cocoons and exploding men flashed through my mind. My voice went equally taut.

"I have," I said.

"That," she said quietly, "is a fraction of what we think can happen if it and the others are together again in the hands of Methuselah."

CHAPTER 29

When Sister Margaret finally stopped speaking, I didn't know whether to scream, walk out, or throw up. All three options seemed valid. All three were far, far preferable to what I now faced—whether I wanted to or not. None, however, would change anything.

Because the stone had bonded to me, to something in me that Sister Margaret had called my magick, which I interpreted as some kind of energetic connection. And the only way I would ever be rid of it was to find Methuselah, die, or at least be as close to death as she had been when she passed it to me. Not, I thought with a shudder, an alternative I wanted to explore, because the slow starvation she'd described going through in an abandoned shed where she'd been trapped? Definitely not on my bucket list.

Although that scenario was unlikely, because I'd already proved my ability to use the stone to decimate my foes, something that Sister Margaret said she hadn't been able to bring herself to do.

Later, I might try to decide what that said about me. Or not.

I might also ask her how she'd escaped and made it to me, but for now, it was enough that, for all intents and purposes, the stone and I were joined at the hip—and the wrist, and the hand, and up my arm, and now that I thought about it, I could feel the spiderweb strands throughout my entire body, and—

I leveled a hard stare at the nun across the table. "That's it? That's all you can tell me? *Here's a magick stone, we're not entirely sure how it works other than you can never get rid of it, good luck?* You must have more information than that, damn it."

"I wish I did. In retrospect, not putting together an archive sooner may not have been our best decision. But—"

"Ya think?" I growled.

"But," Sister Margaret continued, "we thought that it was best not to have everything in one place."

No, I thought sarcastically, *better by far to have it scattered across the globe in thousands of forgotten cellars and attics and caves, in dozens of languages—some of those now* dead *languages—until the alien that knew the stones' full potential and capacity started to lose its mind. So much better.*

But I swallowed the thought before it became actual words, gritted my teeth, and searched for something more constructive. I found little and settled for a third round of trying to understand the key player in all of this. "And Methuselah," I said. "You're sure it's dementia we're dealing with."

"As sure as we can be, given his ... differentness," Margaret dropped her voice on the last word, casting a cautious glance at the occupied tables near us. "The sisters who cared for him said that he's been losing chunks of memories ever since he came to them."

"Chunks?" She hadn't used that word before. "It hasn't been gradual?"

The nun shook her head. "The last episode was when John F. Kennedy was shot. One of the sisters who still cares —cared—for him was there, and she said it was like watching amnesia happen in front of her eyes. He lost so much that day, including his memory of the stones themselves."

"Until ...?" I prompted. I'd be hearing this part for the third time, too, but maybe—just maybe—I'd missed something else, another key word or element. Out of the corner of my eye, I saw Dawson flapping a hand at us, trying to get our attention. I ignored her.

"Until a little over six months ago," Sister Margaret said. "We'd received a message on February 21 from St. Mary's that the last stone had disappeared from—"

"St. Mary's—*my* St. Mary's? *They* had one of the stones?"

"They were the house keeping us in the loop. The stone had been taken from Basel, Switzerland on the nineteenth—and Methuselah walked away from his keepers the next day."

"That part," I said. "Tell me more about that part. Did he say anything? Do anything? Did they try to stop him?"

Margaret pressed her lips together and shrugged her shoulders. "I don't know," she said. "I wish I did. All they said was that he was gone."

I slouched back in my chair. A dull thud hammered at my temples, part exhaustion, part overwhelm, and likely a good part low blood sugar, given that I never did get around to eating my burger and fries. I took the lid off the now-tepid coffee that Dawson had brought over and helped myself to four of the sugar packets she'd dropped on the table. It wasn't much, but it would have to do for now. I'd get a fresh burger on the way out when I ordered Phoenix's meal.

I glanced over at Dawson, who tapped on her wrist in a *time's up* gesture. I held up two fingers in return, and she glowered at me. I turned my attention back to Sister Margaret.

"The stone you gave me," I said, picking up the stir stick the nun had set aside. "You told me you'd found it, but you didn't say where—or how."

Margaret had glossed over that part of the story, and in

view of all the other questions I'd had, I hadn't pressed, but now something nudged at me, telling me I needed to know. Even if it made her gaze turn haunted and her expression go taut with misery.

"I wasn't even looking for it," she said. "I went after Methuselah. There had been a sighting near Toronto—in Oakville. I took the train there and met Sister Ernestine. We searched the entire town for hours without success. Sister Ernestine had to take the vehicle back for an appointment for Sister Juliana, so she dropped me at the train station. I was all set to board when I saw him—or at least, I thought I saw him. I'd never met him, but the description seemed—"

"Dawson is clearing her table," I interrupted. "We need to speed this up."

"I followed. It wasn't him after all, and I got turned around and ended up following the train tracks in the wrong direction into a wooded area, and ..."

"You found the stone."

"I found the cocoon," she corrected. "A man was wrapped in it, and it looked like animals had found him. The terror on his face—"

She broke off and swallowed, then amended, "On what was *left* of his face ..."

"Sweet Mary," I muttered.

"Indeed," said Margaret. She fell silent for a few seconds, and despite Dawson now standing cross-armed beside the door, sending glowering looks in my direction, I didn't have the heart to press her.

At last, the nun straightened her shoulders and picked up her tale. "The stone was still in his hand. I used a corner—"

"Hold on." My hand shot across the table and seized one of hers. "What do you mean, the stone was still in *his* hand? If he had the stone, how could he have been cocooned?"

She looked surprised by my question. "Didn't I tell you? The stones' powers are drawn to dark magick. That's what they're doing when they cocoon someone. He wasn't wearing gloves, and if someone who practices dark magick touches a stone, it binds to them the way yours did to you, but then it—I don't know"—she waved the hand I wasn't holding onto for dear life in a little circle—"feeds off of the darkness? Sucks the darkness and the life out of its victims? We're honestly not sure about that part."

Didn't she tell me? No, she fucking didn't tell me. I wouldn't forget something like that. Something like I had a fucking spiderweb time bomb in my pocket that could wrap me in a cocoon at any moment and suck me dry.

"But you're not at risk," Margaret hastened to assure me, patting the hand still clamped over one of hers. "It only happens to disciples."

"Disciples?" I croaked. My brain, still recovering from the whole dark magick and being sucked dry thing, instantly jumped to Bible stories and threatened to explode again. The patriarchy was one thing, but *disciples*? Surely I'd misheard. Truth be told, I hoped I'd misheard pretty much everything I'd heard today. And yesterday.

"A disciple of magecraft."

And that didn't change my mind.

This was going to take longer than I'd thought, and longer than Dawson wanted.

Releasing my grip on Sister Margaret, I flashed a look out the window at the still-there motel, then at the detective by the door. Dawson stared back at me, rolled her eyes toward the ceiling, and shook her head, then stalked back to her table. Fighting a tremble in my hand, I reached for three more packets of sugar, tore them open, and dumped them into my cup. Healthy, no. Necessary? To quote the late Sister Anne Louise, sweet Moses in a muffin tin, yes.

"Magecraft, I'm guessing, being the practice of the dark magick you mentioned." I swirled the stir stick through cold coffee that now bordered on syrup.

"Exactly," she said. "Think of it as the opposite of witchcraft."

Right, because witchcraft was all about sunshine and rainbows, and holy Mother, when she'd said the stone had bound itself to my magick earlier, she'd meant *actual* magick?

"I'm not sure what the lowest rank is," she continued, frowning in concentration while I tried not to hyperventilate. "The apprentice Mages who are the equivalent of practicing witches, I mean. They're the ones who don't know to protect themselves from the stones when they try to steal them—and the ones who are most likely to think that what I found in the woods won't happen to them." She shivered at the memory.

"By the time they achieve Mage status, they're the equivalent of our midwitches. Master Mages, their most powerful, work with the various factions that would like to control the stones. You might say that magecraft's obsession with the stones is what powers—literally—the entire patriarchy."

"Our—" My hand knocked against the paper cup, slopping coffee across the table and changing my question to a growled, "Fuck!"

The middle-aged couple at the table next to us paused in their conversation and stared at me. With an effort, I refrained from swearing at them as well, summoned an apologetic smile, and waited until their disapproving attention moved away. Then I leaned across the table and lowered my voice to a whisper. Or maybe a hiss.

Either way, it carried the full impact of my shock.

"Our *midwitches*? Are you saying that some of the Obsidian Sisterhood are *witches*?" Was she saying *I* was?

"Yes and no. To stay hidden, to keep the stones safe, the women who join the order vow not to use magick, regardless of their faith or affiliation. We learned long ago that they—the stones—and we were all safest in a non-magickal environment. But mark my words, all of us are very much witches at heart, Sister Monica, whether we want to know it or not."

For a moment, the entire world receded. I could see Sister Margaret's lips continuing to move, and a part of me understood that it meant she was still talking, but I couldn't hear her. I couldn't hear anything but a ringing in my ears, the pulse of blood through my veins, my own shallow breath. I felt like the proverbial rug had been ripped out from under my feet, and I was falling and not stopping. Like there was no stopping.

I wanted to deny the witch revelation—viscerally and with every atom of my being—but I couldn't. I couldn't, because I knew—just as viscerally—that it was true. That it had always been true, at least for me.

Memories rushed in on me, the deeply buried kind that turned everything in the life I'd lived upside down and inside out. My sixth sense, my mother had called it. I remembered that my father had tried to beat it out of me and to replace it with the fear of God and the guilt that were endemic to his faith. Mama had tried to run interference as best she could, but Father had been a hard man, and when Mama died giving birth to my sixth sibling, I had buried my "evilness" alongside her out of sheer, instinctive self-preservation.

Self-preservation and responsibility, because as the oldest, the burden of raising the others—and of protecting the intersex baby my father had called an abomination—had fallen to me. I was twelve.

It was the nuns, led by Mother Joan, who had saved me. Before my mother had even been buried, they had assigned the infant as male and named him Joseph in the hopes that my father would be more accepting of a son. He was not, but the nuns had persevered. They found a nurse for the baby and insisted my father hire a house-keeper so that I could attend school, where they saw to it that I kept up my grades.

When Mother Joan had floated the idea six years later of me joining St. Paul's Monastery as a novice, it had seemed a natural transition. She promised me that monastic life would be no more restrictive than life under my father's roof, and when I expressed concerns about my youngest sibling, she assured me that she would look after him as best she could, and that he would be fine—espe-cially because he had started school and would become part of the community there.

I had been young and naïve enough to want to believe her on both counts—about monastic life and about Joseph—but oh, how wrong she and I had ultimately been.

In truth, I had been wrong about a great many things in my life, mostly because, for too many years, I hadn't known what *my* life was. But now, in just a few words, Sister Margaret had stripped away ...

A veil, I thought. She'd stripped away a veil that I hadn't even known I still wore. A veil between the person that my father and the church had created and the person that was *me*. The me who sat in a fast-food restaurant, on the run from Mages, with a magical stone in her pocket and another nun telling her that she was a witch at heart, and—

"Sister Monica?" Sister Margaret's hand covered mine, pulling my attention back to her. "Are you all right?"

No. No, I was most certainly not all right. In fact, my litany of reasons to not be all right was so long that I didn't even know where to begin, and even if I had …

I looked at the bony wrist protruding from the shirt that hung on the frame of the woman across from me. Her fingers were so thin that their knuckles appeared deformed, and her face looked more like a Halloween mask than a living human. Sister Margaret had lost just as much as I had, I thought. Perhaps more.

Even if I *had* known where to begin, I could not—would not—dump my list of *not-right* on her.

So I straightened my spine, pulled the remains of my steadfastness around me like a somewhat tattered cape, and made myself nod. "Nothing a good night's sleep won't fix," I assured her. "And then tomorrow—"

I broke off, nonplussed. *Hell*, I thought. *I had no idea what I would do tomorrow, because damned if I wasn't back at square one of the no-plan thing.* I pursed my lips and frowned at Sister Margaret.

"I have no idea what to do tomorrow," I said. "Or the next day, for that matter. I'm assuming we need to look for the other stones?"

"Eventually, yes, but we need to find Methuselah first," she replied, pulling her hand back and tucking it beneath the table. "For now, at least, the Mages can't use the stones without destroying themselves."

"And if they find Methuselah?" I prompted.

"With his memory as bad as it is, Methuselah is … fragile. According to his caregivers, over the last several decades, he needed directions for even the most everyday things: getting up, eating, drinking, sleeping. Essentially, unless someone told him what to do, he did nothing."

"But if they did tell him what to do ..."

The nun's expression turned grim. "He did it. Every time."

I puffed up my cheeks and blew out a gust of air in a holy-freaking-Mary kind of way. "He and the stones together—you're certain it would be a bad thing? Would he even remember what to do with them?"

"We're sure it would be an incredibly powerful thing if he did," she said, "and that Earth might not survive. We can't take the risk."

I looked past her shoulder and over the car roof at the traffic whizzing past on the busy street. I would have liked to suggest—to believe—that no one, not even the Mages, would be so stupid as to chance the destruction of the very planet they were on, but in the face of human history, I wasn't that naive. Nor was I particularly hopeful—not about that, and not about our chances of finding one old man that we couldn't even file a missing persons report on because, fucking Methuselah.

I put a hand to my neck and massaged the tightness there as I tipped my head back as far as it would go, then tilted it from side to side. "Right," I said, "so we start with Methuselah, but *where* do we start?"

Sister Margaret sighed. "I honestly have no idea," she said, "If the archive had survived, we might have had a chance at figuring it out. The history in there is so rich— *was* so rich. You're sure the entire room was destroyed? Nothing could have survived?"

All too recent and all too vivid, Sister Anne Louise's scream echoed in my memory. I thought back to the flash of purple light around the edges of the archive door, followed by the explosion, and then the other explosions and the resulting fires and my utter helplessness. I gritted my teeth.

Not about me, I reminded myself.

"I'm sure," I said. "It's gone. Why in hell do they keep blowing things up, anyway? Are they compensating for something?"

Sister Margaret's lips twitched. "Perhaps, but I think the primary reason is fear. They're like any terrorist—they want to create chaos and instability so that they can gain the upper hand."

"So. Definitely compensating."

This time the nun chuckled, then she sighed again. "Well, whatever their reason, perhaps this time, it was for the best, because if anything *did* survive, the Mages would have it now."

"We still have the journal that Phoenix is reading," I said. "Is there *any* possibility there's enough in it to point us in the right direction?"

"Maybe?" She pursed her lips thoughtfully. "Sister Anne Louise had six months to work on it after I left, and I have no doubt she would have focused her efforts on Methuselah, but her eyes weren't very good anymore. Working for more than a couple of hours a day was all she could manage, and you saw the room. There was so much to read through."

I'd seen, all right. There had been enough material in that cellar room to keep several Sister Anne Louises busy for several years ... and then some. I glanced out the window at the motel again, its façade a mix of shadows and reflected light now that night had settled.

A lull in the general noise of the restaurant caught my attention, and I turned my head and looked over my shoulder. Patrons and staff alike were staring out the window on the other side of the vestibule doors, poking at one another and pointing outside. I craned my neck, but I couldn't see whatever was causing the ripple of excitement.

"I'll have a look when we get back to the motel," Sister Margaret continued as if oblivious to the stir. "Phoenix and I can compare notes, and—"

She broke off as Dawson suddenly loomed tableside, arm brushing my nose as she pointed past me and out the window.

"What the fuck," the detective snarled, "is that?"

CHAPTER 30

THAT, I DECIDED AS I FOLLOWED DAWSON'S POINTING finger to the creature in the parking lot outside the restaurant, was a monster. It was the only word I had for it. And it was massive.

At least ten feet tall and built like a small mountain, it stood in a puddle of light below a streetlamp, swaying on what looked like haunches carved of granite. Patches of sparse fur sprouted from it in some places, and lichens covered others. Its hands were the size of boulders, and it had a long face like a dog's muzzle, with dog-ears set back on its skull and blank, beady eyes that scanned the restaurant windows as if searching for something.

The restaurant patrons lined up along the windows and in front of the door, phone cameras pointed at the mountain as they jostled for a better look, a better shot. Someone yelled at someone else not to push, a child wailed for their mother, the couple at the table next to ours began praying loudly, a man shouted that the police were on their way.

"Sister Margaret?" Dawson asked, her voice terse.

"No idea," responded my nun companion. "But I'm guessing that it belongs to the Mages."

I'd come to the same conclusion, because the thing had to have materialized out of thin air. No one in the restaurant had noticed its approach. If they had, someone would have—

I flinched as a woman near me screeched. That. Someone would have done that, but a lot sooner. Voices jumbled together in a buzz of excitement and alarm as the mountain shambled closer to the restaurant and lowered its head to peer inside. Oh, yes. It was definitely looking for something, all right, and my money—what little I had of it —was on the stone that pulsed against my hip bone. But if the Mages had brought it here, where were the Mages?

A man crowded closer on my left, and his elbow caught me just above my ear as he banged on the window to get the mountain's attention. "Here!" he shouted through the glass, pointing his phone camera at it. "Over here!"

The deformed dog-head swiveled in his direction—in our direction—and the boulder-hands curled into fists. Cold crawled across my skin, and the stone's pulse rate accelerated. Or maybe that was mine. Either way—

A hand settled on my shoulder, and I jumped.

Dawson leaned down. "Is it after the stone?" she asked.

"Yes. No. I don't know." But I didn't dare stay here to find out. I shrugged off her hand and pushed back my chair, ignoring the outraged squawk from the man who'd elbowed me as I stood and scanned the restaurant for the fastest way out. There was undoubtedly a back or side door, but if I were going to draw whatever the hell that was away, I needed it to see me leave. Needed it to—

I stopped mid-thought as I looked back out the window, and the small mountain's beady gaze locked onto mine. For long seconds, we stared at one another. Then creature tipped back its head and pointed its muzzle toward the night sky, and then it howled. Or roared. Or maybe screamed.

Whatever you wanted to call the sound, it was hoarse and raw and primal, and it slammed against the windows, making the glass vibrate and the restaurant patrons gasp and take a collective step back.

A fresh surge of adrenaline hit my bloodstream, and I surged to my feet. Was that a challenge? A call to arms for others like it? An announcement to the Mages that it had found me? I didn't know—and I didn't have time to wait and see. I had to get the creature away from here. *Now.* Away from these people, to where I could limit the damage it—and I—might inflict. As the monster's scream died away, I whirled and grabbed Dawson's arm.

"Keep everyone inside," I ordered. "And whatever you do, don't follow—"

"It's leaving!" said the same man who'd banged on the window—and then he did it again, striking the glass with the flat of his hand for maximum noise. "Hey! Hey, over here! Come back!"

"Fucking moron," muttered Dawson. She pulled free of my grip and reached past me to grab the man, barking at him to sit down and shut up.

Leaving her to deal with him and everyone else, I shouldered my way through the crowd toward the door. I'd taken only three or four steps when Dawson's shout made me freeze.

"Shit! The motel. Monica, it's heading for the—"

I didn't hear the rest. With utter disregard for those I shoved out of my way, I barreled through the remainder of the patrons to the door and pushed my way outside. I stumbled to a halt, my frantic gaze searching the parking lot, the street—

The motel parking lot across the street.

The mountain was already there. Already striding toward the building. Already reaching up to tear at the veranda before the door to room 213. For a moment, I watched in horror, unable to make my legs move, as aluminum and wood peeled away from the building in sheets and chunks and splinters. Then a boulder-fist drew back and slammed into the door. Our door. Mine and Phoenix's.

Phoenix, whose own scream mingled with another roar

from the mountain and spurred me at last to action. Staggering forward on legs that felt like they were made of lead and fused to the pavement, I yelled for the mountain's attention and dug frantic fingers into my pocket, trying to find the stone. But my voice was lost in a cacophony of noise—the monster's roar, Phoenix's screams, the honking of horns and screech of tires, the wail of approaching sirens—and the stone kept slipping from my grasp.

I wound my way between stopped cars and the people who had exited them to gawk at the unfolding drama, yelling until my throat ached and my voice turned hoarse. The mountain remained oblivious, and the stone—the *fucking* stone—continued to elude me.

And then the mountain pulled Phoenix from the ruined motel room and held her aloft like a rag doll, Dawson barreled past me with gun drawn, and a huge purple fireball smashed into the wreckage.

CHAPTER 31

FEAR," SISTER MARGARET HAD TOLD ME WHEN I'D ASKED why the Mages kept blowing things up. *"Like any terrorist, they want to create chaos and instability."*

Well, it was working.

Grimly, I pulled myself up from the ground, using the side mirror of the car I'd been thrown against. Someone reached out to help me, but I shook them off. The street and parking lot were chaos, with people shouting and milling about and calling for help for the injured, and the motel...

I shuddered as I took in the inferno that raged where the motel had stood only seconds before. The Mages were getting bolder. For my benefit?

It seemed likely, but I wasn't going to dwell on the possibility. Not right now, when I had only thought in mind. One concern. Phoenix.

"Sister Monica! Oh, thank God you're all right." Sister Margaret's hands brushed at the dust covering my shirt, then felt along my shoulders and arms. "You *are* all right? Nothing is broken?"

I shook her off as I had the previous helping hands. "I'm fine. But Phoenix?"

The nun made no effort to prevaricate. "It took her," she said simply. "It covered her with its body when the explosion hit, and then it took her."

My heart dropped into my toes, and for a moment, my lungs refused to draw air. Sweet Mary, not Phoenix, too. I'd already lost so many—the other shelter residents, my sisters at St. Mary's … Joseph who had been Josephine all along. I wouldn't, couldn't lose—

"The journal," Sister Margaret said, breaking into my angst as she grabbed my arm again. This time she refused to let go. "It may have taken the journal, too, Monica."

My throat went tight. Holy hell. I'd forgotten about the journal.

"You have to get it back," the nun continued. "It's all we have—"

"I know," I interrupted.

Sister Margaret's mouth snapped shut, but her grip tightened, and I could almost see the words hovering on her lips. Words I did not want and could not bear to hear.

"I *know*," I growled again, and I did. I knew that if I found the monster and Phoenix, I might face a choice. An unthinkable, impossible choice. I knew, and Margaret knew, and I hoped to the holy Mother herself that we were both wrong, because if it came down to it, I didn't know what my choice would be.

Phoenix, my heart whispered.

"This isn't about you," the memory of Sister Margaret's voice replied.

The here-and-now sister pressed her lips together and nodded. "I know you do," she said, releasing my arm and stepping back. "Now go. I'll find Detective Dawson.".

My heart dropped a second time. Dawson. I'd forgotten all about Dawson. She'd just run past me, gun in hand, when—

Out in the night, the monster screamed again, its voice fainter that it had been, but still easily heard even over the arriving sirens, the cries of pain and terror, and the roar of flames—at least until the blast of a truck's air horn swallowed it.

My head snapped around a second time as, Dawson

again forgotten, I zeroed in on the sound. I cringed when I saw the headlights whizzing past in both directions on the highway between me and it.

The damned thing had gone and crossed the fucking 401.

THE MOTEL DAWSON HAD BOOKED US INTO AND THE FAST-food restaurant we'd vacated across from it were two of a handful of buildings that occupied a service road running alongside the MacDonald-Cartier Freeway, better known as Highway 401. The freeway held the dubious honor of being North America's busiest where it ran through Toronto, and while this stretch of it outside Kingston ran through miles of forest and was much quieter traffic-wise, it was still—

I flinched at the passing of a transport truck, then another, then another. The vortices left in their wakes sucked at me, whipping my shirt up into my face and making me stagger—and underlining my incomplete thought.

Because as a major transportation corridor, the highway was still fucking dangerous, and attempting to cross its six lanes was just plain foolhardy. Especially in the dark. But if the monster had crossed here and taken Phoenix with it, I would have to cross, too.

At least there were only three lanes to cross at a time. Small blessings, right?

Steeling myself, I tucked my shirt into the waistband of my jeans and settled into a crouch. Headlights streamed toward me, then past me as I waited for a break in traffic.

There wasn't one. Transport trucks thundered by, one after another, some of them blasting their horns at me, but none of them slowing. My presence here would have already been reported to the Ontario Provincial Police that patrolled the highway, I was sure. There was probably already a cop on the—

My mouth tightened as I glimpsed the flash of blue and red lights in the distance. Shit. I hesitated, debating returning the way I'd come—at least far enough to hide in the brush at the edge of the highway corridor—but over the rumble of another truck, I heard the monster's roar again. Faint, but undeniable.

I was going forward, not back.

I glanced at the distant police car lights, then put their approach out of my mind and focused again on the traffic. Truck after truck after car after truck, with no break in sight. A part of me wanted to scream in frustration, but I gritted my teeth against it. Focus turned to hyperfocus, and then—

There. The stillness I'd been unable to find earlier was there now, at my core where it had always been, solid and reassuring this time instead of elusive. Waiting for me. I exhaled a long, slow breath and settled into it, my gaze on the steady stream of headlights. *You can do this*, the stillness whispered to me. *You must.*

Truck ... truck ... *inhale* ... truck ... car ... *exhale*—

Three lanes, the meridian, three more lanes. The stillness was right. I could—

Now, it urged. *Run now.*

I didn't hesitate. I sprinted across the pavement, fighting to stay upright in the turbulence of the last truck that whipped past and racing for my very life against the next. An air horn blasted, once, twice, a third time. Calmly, fiercely, I kept my eyes on the wide, grassy meridian that was my goal.

Hail Mary Magdalene, full of grace, come and sit with me.

A truck's emergency brakes screamed, and the corresponding squeal of tires against asphalt filled my ears as I crossed the first dividing line between lanes. Brilliant lights bore down on me from the left, then skewed away as the truck they belonged to jackknifed across the highway and slid sideways toward me. Fresh adrenaline shot through my veins.

Fuck sitting, I told my patron saint. *Come and run with me —and please don't let me be the cause of someone else's accident tonight.*

Reaching deep, I summoned a speed I'd never before achieved and crossed the second lane, then the third. The rough pavement of the rumble strip beneath my feet marked the shoulder, and I lengthened my stride, took two giant steps, and threw myself into the wide, shallow ditch that divided the east and west-bound lanes of the freeway. I tucked instinctively into a roll as momentum carried me toward a face plant —and then, on the verge of offering thanks to my patron saint for my safe arrival, I instead swore mightily as I came to rest in a soft, marshy spot that smelled like something had died in it.

Clambering to my feet, I slogged through the soft muck that sucked at my running shoes, dropped to all fours to climb the short, gentle slope on the other side, and staggered upright again at the top. Traffic on this side crawled along at a fraction of the speed limit. Drivers slowed to look at the jackknifed truck I'd left behind me, and the blue and red lights I'd seen in the distance splashed their reflection across the side of a white semi-trailer. An accompanying siren *whooped* three times in quick succession.

I had no doubt that it was meant for me, but I paid no

attention. I dodged around the semi, waited for a pickup to pass, ignored the angry gesticulations of the driver as I ignored the police car, and then darted into the woods. There, I paused for a moment to look back.

Flames from the burning motel lit up the night sky on the other side of the freeway I'd crossed, and the lights of a dozen emergency vehicles lined the street between restaurant and inferno, where I'd left Sister Margaret searching for Detective Dawson. Across the eastbound lanes of the freeway itself sat the jackknifed truck, with dozens of other vehicles already lined up behind it—and more coming. The OPP car was stuck in the marshy spot I'd found, the officer had bailed out of it and was talking on his radio, and I could hear the wail of at least one more siren approaching from the east.

It was, in a word, chaos.

I turned and walked away from it.

CHAPTER 32

I FOUND PHOENIX A HUNDRED YARDS INTO THE WOODS, though it may have been more accurate to say that I almost tripped over her.

I'd been so focused on not falling flat on my face or walking into a tree that I hadn't been paying much attention to anything beyond the immediate. In retrospect and given what I was trailing, that probably wasn't smart, but to be fair, I wasn't expecting a hazard to grab me by the ankle, either. When it did, I gave a most unheroic squawk, slapped my hand over my mouth to muffle the sound, and fell onto my backside beside—

"Sister?" whispered the crumpled-up figure at the base of a massive tree. It was barely visible in the shadows. "Is that you?"

My heart did a dozen backflips as the voice registered and the form took shape. "Phoenix?" I scrambled toward her on all fours. "Phoenix! Are you all right?"

She sat with knees drawn up to her chest, and I caught my breath on a groan as I got close enough to make out her features. Her face was battered almost beyond recognition. Tear tracks ran through the dried blood on her cheeks, and she had to twist her head to one side to peer at me through the slit of an eye that was swollen almost shut.

The other eye already was.

Nausea rolled in my stomach. "Sweet Mary," I whispered. I reached for her with gentle hands. "Oh, Phoenix—"

But she pushed me away. "No," she said, shaking her head. "No, Sister. You have to go after them. I tried to keep it from them, but they took it and then they left, and I couldn't follow them because I couldn't see right, and—"

"Hush," I said, brushing aside her hands and reaching for her again, because oh, Mother of All, her face. Her poor, poor face. "It's okay, Phoenix."

She shoved harder, almost knocking me onto my butt again. "It's *not* okay. They have the journal, Sister. There are things in there—Sister Anne Louise wrote things—you have to get it back!"

I hesitated, torn between looking after her and going after—who? And go where? Apart from the little enclave of buildings where the motel sat—had sat—forest dominated the landscape for miles along this part of the 401. Whoever had taken the journal could have gone anywhere. Further into the woods on foot, or back to the highway and a waiting car …

Well. Except maybe for the mountain of a monster. It, at least, was still roaming through the trees somewhere. And if I did leave to go after the journal, it might come back to finish what it had started with Phoenix.

A shudder ran through me, and cold settled into my core. This was it, I thought. This was the choice that Sister Margaret and I had both understood I might have to make. It was every bit as impossible as I'd feared. I closed my eyes and pressed my lips together between my teeth until they became painful, but it didn't make it any easier.

Phoenix tugged at my sleeve. "Sister Monica? Did you hear me?"

I opened my eyes again and took in all that I could see in the dark of my brave, beautiful girl. "You said *they*. How many of them are there?"

"Two. The man and the monster—he called it a goliath. I don't think it likes him very much. It screams every time he tells it to do something, but it still does what he wants."

Goliath? As in David and —? I pushed away the name and my questions about it until later—if there was a later —and focused on getting more information. If I was going to run off in pursuit of that thing and what was most certainly a Mage, I needed to know everything Phoenix could remember. "And the man?"

"He looked familiar, but I don't know where I know him from. As soon as he saw the journal, he made the goliath take it from me and give it to him. Then he told it that they didn't need me anymore and to—to—" Phoenix broke off into a cross between a hiccup and a sob, and it took all the strength I could muster not to push past her objections, fold her against me, and hold her.

Phoenix took a deep breath and squared her shoulders. "It brought me here," she continued, "and then it ... disappeared."

"It didn't go with the man?"

She shook her head. "No. There was a kind of light— it looked like a ribbon—that swallowed it, and"—she shrugged—"it sorta went poof."

I wasn't at all sure that *poof* was a good thing, because it seemed to me that what had *poofed* away could *poof* back again, but at least the mountain was gone for now, and that was a good thing. It didn't make my decision to leave Phoenix here and go after the journal much easier, but it helped. I sat back on my heels.

"Right," I said. "Can you walk?"

Phoenix nodded. "I think so."

"Good. The highway is that way"—I pointed in the direction I'd come from, waiting to be sure her gaze followed in the dark before I continued—"and there are police already there. They may even be in the woods by now, looking for me. As soon as you can hear voices, start yelling for help and let them come to you. They'll take you to Sister Margaret and Detective Dawson. Understand?"

Assuming there still was a Detective Dawson to take her to.

I shut that thought away with all the others I didn't have time to deal with as Phoenix nodded a second time.

"Good," I said again, as much to convince myself as to reassure her. I pushed up to my feet and held out a hand to help her up from the ground. "Now, which way did they go?"

My beautiful, brave girl didn't even hesitate. "That way," she said, lifting her bruised chin defiantly and pointing away from the highway and into the woods. "I heard branches snapping that way."

As it turned out, "branches snapping that way" wasn't a lot to go on, especially in the dark.

But a faint glimmer of light through the trees? That was something, even when it disappeared again. Or perhaps because it did, because it suggested to me that whoever carried it was trying to hide it.

I paused in pushing through the underbrush and stared at the spot I'd last seen the light. Whether by accident or divine chance—I tended to think those were one and the same, most days—I had stumbled on a quasi-path of sorts almost as soon as I'd left Phoenix and gone to the edge of the parking lot. It wasn't much—a deer trail, perhaps, or one made by an adventurous motel guest— but it led me deep enough into the trees that the flames from the burning motel had become a faint glow, and I could no longer see the tall, overly bright parking lot lights.

Which made the glimmer in the trees all the more promising—and there it was again. Moving to the left, then the right, then stopping … and remaining stopped. It was no more than fifty feet away, but in the dark and silence of the night that closed around me, it might as well have been a dozen miles off, because there was no way I could approach it with any measure of stealth. I took a deep breath and crept forward as quietly as I—

A twig snapped beneath my foot, sending a sharp *crack* into the stillness.

I dropped into a crouch and froze.

The light in the woods didn't move.

Cautiously, I stood up again and watched it for another few seconds. It remained, steady and constant. I rolled my shoulders. My injured one objected, but it was a half-hearted protest at best. Despite the demands I continued to make of it—including wandering through the woods in the dark—my body was beginning to heal. Either that, or it had just given up complaining.

One at a time, I shook out my hands, my arms, my legs, releasing the tension that had gathered as I'd tried not to fall over various roots and stumps. The light remained. Almost, I amended my earlier assessment, as if whoever it belonged to wasn't trying to hide after all but was instead waiting for me. Waiting for a fight.

I straightened my spine. So be it. I wasn't getting any younger standing out here, and if they'd underestimated me before, maybe they would do so again. At least I was wiser to their tricks and knew what to expect—from them *and* from me.

As long as their mountain stayed *poofed*, of course.

I pressed my lips together, took a deep breath, and strode forward.

I FOUND THE LIGHT IN A CLEARING THAT WAS NO MORE than twenty feet in diameter. It hovered a few feet in the air, white and pulsing slowly, casting the trees around the perimeter into dark relief. A man was there, too. He sat on a boulder in the center of the open space, one leg crossed over the opposite knee, and the open journal resting against it. His head was bent over it as if he were reading.

There was no sign of the mountain.

I brushed a twig from my hair as I stepped out of the woods and regarded him. He gave no sign of having heard me crashing through the trees, and he might as well have been sitting in a library—he was that unperturbed. I cleared my throat.

The man held up a single finger, instructing me to wait. I raised an eyebrow. Seriously?

"You're joking," I said. "You dragged me out here to watch you read? I don't think so."

He took his time closing the book, leaving it lying on his leg as he looked up at me. "I didn't drag you anywhere," he replied. "Following me out here was your idea, not mine." His voice was deep and melodious, and in the light from the sphere floating above him, I thought I detected a twinkle of humor in his eyes.

"Perhaps. But stealing my journal"—I nodded at the book he held—"was *your* idea."

He glanced down at it and ran a hand over its leather cover. A gloveless hand, I noticed, which meant that he was either one of the beginners Sister Margaret had mentioned, or that he wasn't after my stone. The first possibility seemed unlikely, because his air of confidence spoke of control and power.

The second possibility sent a frisson of caution down my spine, because if not the stone, then what?

He looked up at me again, then rose from the boulder and turned to set the book down gently in the spot he'd vacated. Then he faced me, and the full light of the sphere fell across his face. I drew a startled breath. Was that really—?

"Eldon Rusk," confirmed the man I'd recognized as one of the most influential billionaires in the word. He gave me a formal half-bow. "I'd say *at your service*, but we both know I'd be lying. Just as you are lying about that being your journal, because the law of possession says that it's mine, now." Sliding his hands into his pants pockets, he added, "Just as the stone that you carry will be mine, along with all the others."

Caution became outright foreboding. "You have the others?"

"My partners and I have them, yes."

"A consortium," I said. "Made up of whom?"

"Ooh. Nice use of grammar. Consortium *and* whom." He inclined his head. "You're an educated woman."

Rich, influential, and a prick.

"You haven't answered."

"And I'm not going to. For two reasons." Eldon Rusk held up a hand and extended his thumb. "One, it's none of your business. And two"—his other hand rose with thumb also extended—"as soon as I have the keeper of the stones, it won't matter, because I'll be the one in control."

I wasn't sure what was more terrifying: his supreme confidence or knowing that, if he did find Methuselah, he'd be right. "But why?" I asked. "What good can possibly come of that kind of control when you might destroy the entire planet?"

"I might," he agreed, "Or I might not. Life is all about risk, haven't you heard? But of course you have, or else you wouldn't be out here. You risked everything to follow me—your friends, your life, the stone you're trying to protect—all without knowing what the outcome would be. You might win and retrieve the journal, or—" he shrugged again and chuckled. "Spoiler alert: You might not."

Rusk's hands had remained outstretched, and I noticed that his thumbs had, too. And that his fingers were uncurling to join them. Fire, I thought grimly. He was going to summon fire, but this time, I would be ready.

I slid my own fingers into my pocket and curled my hand around the stone's familiar outline. It sat against my palm, cool and smooth, waiting. Around the clearing, the trees whispered as a breeze passed through them. Rusk's fingers slowly opened and half closed, as if he were massaging the air. No flames appeared. There wasn't so much as a spark. My unease increased. The trees whispered more loudly. Rusk's smile widened.

I scowled. I didn't know what his game was, but I didn't like it, and I was done playing. I pulled my hand and the stone from my pocket, and the familiar spider webs began winding around and through me. "You know you can't take the stone from me," I said.

"Not while you're alive, no." He flexed his hands again, and now his fingers moved like they were typing on an invisible keyboard. "But you don't get to where I am in life without learning a little patience, Sister Monica Barrett, and I've learned to be very patient."

"I haven't," I retorted. "I'm old and tired and cranky, so it's time to give me my journal back and call it a night."

The billionaire Mage tipped back his head and laughed in delight. Because that was what he was. I could feel it in my bones, my very core. Eldon Rusk was unquestionably a Mage—or perhaps even one of the Master Mages that Sister Margaret had mentioned. Calm, confident, supremely in control—and irritating as fuck.

I glowered at him. I really, really didn't want to have to call on the stone again, damn it. I hated that I was being forced into this. Hated that I had become tied to a power as dark as the stone's. Hated that the world had descended to such a level that a nun—former or otherwise—who had spent a lifetime helping others now found herself exploding them instead.

I lifted my hand to brush at a tickle on my cheek. And I really, really hated—

My thoughts faltered. I lifted my hand …

… lifted …

… lift …

I transferred my scowl from Rusk to the hand that was refusing to comply, and my breath left my lungs in a wheeze, because what I really, really hated? Spiders. I hated spiders.

And I was covered in them.

CHAPTER 33

If it had just been the spiders covering me, I might have stood a chance. I might have been able to brush them off, to run from them, to raise my arms away from my body and fight. But it wasn't just the spiders. It was also the cocoon that they had already woven around me.

The silken strands, strong as steel, that tied my feet to the ground and my hands to my sides. That wrapped around my legs, around my torso … around the hand that held the stone. Strands that held me captive as hundreds of thousands of other spiders poured out of the woods, dropping from the trees and rushing across the clearing with a whispering sound that I knew now had nothing to do with a breeze.

For a moment, my mind parted company with my body, standing separate and away, watching the spiders spinning and crawling, crawling and spinning. Watching the cocoon encase my shoulders, then my neck. Watching Rusk's fingers move faster and faster, and then—

Then they stilled.

Not the spiders. Those continued their weaving work, with more reinforcements arriving with every passing second. But Rusk's fingers stilled, and he shook out his hands and dropped them to his sides as he walked over to stand before me. The sphere of light followed him, sitting just above his shoulder, and my mind jolted back into my body.

Now, it whispered. *Use the stone now.*

I tried. I tried everything. I willed it, I wriggled my fingers as much as their cocoon would allow, I visualized the webs spreading through my hand and then through the—

Realization hit like the original crowbar that had started this odyssey, smashing into me hard enough to knock me to the ground. Or so I wished. Because that was the missing element. The earth. The times that the stone had worked, I'd been flat on my face, connected with the earth—or at least a floor. The spiderwebs from the stone had spread from it through the hand that touched the ground ... as if the earth itself had become some kind of giant antenna that magnified the magick.

The earth that I was now separated from and would never touch again.

Rusk's fingers poked between the strands of web encasing my neck, and he lifted my chin until I met his gaze. Until he stared into my anger, my frustration, my terror.

"Good," he said softly. "You understand."

I did. It would have been hard not to.

I had committed what one of my senseis had called the cardinal sin of martial arts: I had underestimated my opponent. I'd gotten cocky. And now, now I was going to—

"Die," Rusk agreed cheerfully, as if he'd read my thoughts. "You're going to die." Then he frowned. "The issue, of course, is that we don't know how long that will take. The stone could keep you alive for days, weeks, months ..." He must have seen something in my eyes, the only part of me still able to move, because he stopped and raised an eyebrow.

"You didn't know about the symbiosis? The stone gives as much as it takes—assuming that you're in its good books, that is. The fact you've survived it so far would indicate that you are, so—" He shrugged. "Now we wait. As I've said, I'm a patient man, so I'll come back this way every few

months to check on you, and in the meantime, I have that"
—without looking, he tipped his head back, in the direction
of the journal he'd left on the boulder—"to keep me busy."

Despite the impossibility of my situation, I felt a tiny
hope leap in my chest. If he needed the journal and
expected it to keep him busy for months, then he didn't
have all the other stones—or Methuselah—yet. The tiny
hope sputtered out, because *yet* was the key word—
followed by *situation*, followed by *impossible*.

Because the spiders had encased my mouth and nose
now, and I couldn't draw air through their cocoon, and
they were scurrying up and down from cheekbones to
eyebrows as if weaving a veil across my eyes, and Rusk was
letting go of my chin and stepping back, and—

And then I would have caught my breath, if breathing
had still been a thing, because through the thin spider
gauze covering my eyes, I saw something move. Something
that wasn't Rusk. Something—someone—that was
swinging an impressively large stick at his head ... and
connecting.

The cocoon over my ears muffled the *thwack*, but I still
rejoiced at the sound. At least for the one point three
seconds it took for Rusk to stagger, stumble, and then fall
against me, carrying me to the ground beneath him and
knocking what little oxygen remained from my lungs.

I surfaced to hands tearing sticky spider gauze away
from my face in chunks—and to Dawson's voice swearing a
blue streak above me.

"Jesus, Jesus, Jesus," she was yelling—not just saying,
but yelling, "why did it have to be goddamn spiders? I
fucking *hate* spiders!"

Welcome to the club, I thought hazily. And then, as clarity
returned, my brain added, *Dawson. Dawson is alive.*

More chunks of gauze parted company with my skin, freeing my nose and mouth. I opened the latter and sucked in a deep, glorious breath of air, not caring that I probably inhaled a half dozen live spiders with it. Because dear sweet Mary, Dawson was alive.

I wanted to throw my arms around her in a hug, but those were still pinned to my sides by the cocoon wrapped around my entire body. For now, just knowing she and Phoenix had both survived—that I hadn't lost anyone else—was enough. Smiling, I watched her shadow above me and listened to her mutter on.

"Fucking earwigs would have been better," Dawson continued, oblivious to my return to consciousness. "Cockroaches would have been better, for fucksake!"

"Holy Mother, no," I croaked. "Cockroaches are *never* better."

Dawson shrieked, then smacked my shoulder. "Don't *do* that. You scared the shit out of me." She sat back on her heels and picked up a small but powerful flashlight from the ground, then pointed its beam at my face.

My eyes snapped shut against the glare and I turned my head away.

"Do what?" I groused, tugging at my hands without success. "Breathe? You would have noticed if you weren't so busy ranting about spiders. Some badass cop you are."

"Ranting—I was saving your *ass*, thank you very much. And for the record, this?"

The light's glare dimmed, and I cracked open one eye to see Dawson waving an encompassing hand above her head.

"*None* of this," she growled, "was covered in any kind of training *I* took."

A giggle-snort burst from me. "Me, neither," I admitted. Then I turned my head again, this time in search of my downed foe.

"If you're looking for the spiders, they're gone." Dawson set the flashlight back on the ground and resumed pulling at the cocoon, working now to free my right hand, the stone still clamped within it. "And if you're looking for the asshole, he's out cold over there."

She lifted one hand to point, and I followed the direction of her shadowy finger toward an even more shadowy lump on the ground near the boulder.

"Any idea who he is?" she asked, returning to her task.

"Would you believe Eldon Rusk?"

Her hands stilled. The light was too far away for me to see much of her dark face above me, but I had no trouble imagining the expression on it.

"Eldon Rusk," she repeated. "You're shitting me."

I let silence be my answer. After a few seconds, she went back to her task.

"The OPP are gonna love this," she muttered, referring to the Ontario Provincial Police, who had jurisdiction in this area.

"Speaking of the police, where are they, anyway? Didn't they come with you?"

"I didn't invite them."

"Meaning?"

"Meaning they wanted to wait for a tracking dog, and I didn't."

"So they let you through?"

"So I didn't ask permission. And before you ask, I lost my cell phone somewhere along the way, so I haven't been able to call. Once I get you free, you can walk back to the highway. You'll probably meet them on the way, and then you can bring them here. I'll make sure Bozo over there stays asleep until you get back."

"No," I said. "You go. I'll wait with Rusk."

"You're forgetting which one of us is the cop."

"And you're forgetting what he's capable of," I said quietly.

Dawson fell silent, and a moment later, I felt her pull away the last of the cocoon tying my arm to my body. The stone dropped from my numb fingers to the ground beside me, and I flexed my hand in an effort to restore circulation while she leaned over me and started working on my other arm. When I had some feeling back in my hand, I struggled up to a sitting position, intending to take over from her—or at least help.

But as I reached across myself, movement caught the corner of my eye. My head jerked around in time to see Rusk lunge up from the ground and throw himself at the boulder ... and the journal sitting on it.

I REACTED WITHOUT THOUGHT. IN AN INSTANT, I'D snatched the stone up from its resting spot, bellowed at Dawson to get out of the way, and slammed my fist onto the ground. I knew what to expect this time, or at least, I thought I did. But the speed—

The speed left me breathless. The stone's spider strands wound around and through my hand, snarled around my wrist, climbed my arm. The ground buckled beneath Dawson, and she threw herself to the side, grabbing her flashlight as she rolled away. She shined the beam toward Rusk in time for me to see him snatch the journal off the boulder and look over his shoulder toward me with such malevolence that my heart skipped a beat. Then he was sketching something in the air with his right hand and yelling something I couldn't understand, and—

And holy Mother of All.

I gaped at the long, thin light that stretched across the clearing between him and me—Phoenix had been right, it looked a bit like a ribbon—and then at the mountain emerging from it. The mountain that lifted a foot and slammed it down, on top of my webs that writhed beneath the ground. Behind and to its left, Rusk cackled with utter glee as the fingers of his free hand began to dance again, the way they had when he'd summoned the spiders the first time.

As if I would give them a second chance at—

"Fuck!" bellowed Dawson.

Shit, my brain responded. I didn't need to look at her to confirm what I already knew—that Rusk's attack this time was aimed at her rather than me. That the spiders had returned, and they had begun to cover her. The stone in my hand bucked against my hold as if trying to escape me, and I tightened my fingers until they ached with strain, fighting to hold on to it. The mountain brought its other foot down on top of more webs, stopping their advance toward the Mage.

"Fuck!" Dawson cried again. "Fuck, fuck, *fu*—"

Her voice choked off into silence.

Fury and fear clawed at my chest in equal parts. Instinctively, I seized on them, letting them spread through my mind, and then, taking a deep breath, let myself drop beneath them. Beneath my panic. Beneath my connection to the stone. Beneath myself.

I dropped, and dropped, and fell into the stillness, and breathed, and—

The mountain threw back its head and screamed as the webs emerged from the ground to wind around its legs.

Behind and to its left, Rusk yelled something at it, but his voice was lost in his monster's. Through the haze of heat that had begun to consume me, I watched him run forward and try to grasp the mountain's arm, but the creature shook him off, throwing him to the ground a dozen feet away as it tore at the webs climbing its torso.

Then, even as Rusk pushed up to his feet again, the webs—my webs—dropped away from the mountain and snaked toward him instead, encircling his ankles and tying them to the earth. He staggered and fell to his knees, and the strands snaked around his waist and chest, climbed toward his face, extended down his arm toward the journal, and wrapped around that, too.

"The journal!" Dawson cried. Despite the ferocity of the stone's power that filled me, I felt my heart give a little leap. She was alive, and—

I turned my head to see her tearing at the spiderwebs —the real ones—that had begun to encase her. Begun to, but not fully, because with Rusk's lack of attention, the spiders had retreated again, and Dawson was already half untangled. She looked around at me.

"The journal," she said, tearing at the webs. "You have to save it!"

I would have liked to. Sweet Mary, how I would have liked to. But just as before, I was no longer in control of my own body. I was tied to the ground on one side, the rest of me was still cocooned—and then the heat started.

Holy Mother of All, the heat. I knew what it was now, and that I would survive it, but the knowledge did nothing to alleviate the agony of feeling like I was being burned alive. And then I remembered that, at the internet café, somehow, I had stopped it. I closed my eyes and turned my attention inward, into the heat, into the stone.

Hail Mary Magdalene, full of grace, come and sit with me, I began, but Dawson broke my concentration almost immediately.

"Fuck!" she yelled.

I forced my eyes open to see what was wrong—and instantly wished I hadn't, because while I might have felt like I was on fire, Rusk actually was—and Dawson was stumbling toward him, cobwebs trailing in her wake. Her determined face was illuminated by his flames, and she shielded her face with one hand and reached with the other toward the journal. I opened my mouth to call out, but no sound emerged past the stone's hold on me.

A guttural roar shook the clearing, and then the ground beneath me trembled as the mountain that I had forgotten about took two giant strides toward the Mage and my friend. I watched in horror as it swept up the detective in a massive boulder-hand and turned its back on me, and in greater horror as the heat building inside me erupted outward to envelope everything in the clearing.

Rusk and the journal exploded in a shower of sparks.

CHAPTER 34

I jumped at the sound of Dawson's voice and looked up from my seat on the bench overlooking Lake Ontario. I'd chosen this one over two others in the little park I'd walked to from our hotel so that I could watch the sun rise. The gold and orange and pink sky had not disappointed, but I'd had little appreciation for it. I was too caught up in memories of friends who had died, and of purple fireballs and monsters called goliaths, and—

I scooted over to make room for Dawson. Her intrusion was honestly welcome, and not just because she'd broken the endless loop of my thoughts. With a murmur of thanks, I took the cardboard drink tray with two steaming paper cups that she held out and set it on the bench beside me. She eased herself down at the other end with a little hiss of pain. I pretended not to hear.

By unspoken mutual agreement, we weren't talking about the injuries sustained in the woods the night before last. We asked for help if we needed it—such as when she'd needed a bottle of water opened because of her broken wrist—but that was it. We were fine, we told anyone who asked. And I supposed we would be, eventually.

Right now, however, pretty much everything hurt—and that worried me. It worried me a lot, because if Eldon Rusk had been telling the truth about the stones being in the hands of the consortium—

"Well?" Dawson said, reminding me that I hadn't answered her question.

I grimaced. "Do you want the truth, or would you prefer a platitude?"

She grunted. "I'll consider that answer enough." She nodded at the coffees in the tray between us. "Yours is the one with the 'x' on it. I only put two sugars in it, but you have to promise to eat today. Otherwise, I have six more packets in my pocket."

I chuckled at the threat. "You have my word."

She tried to pry the sippy lid open on her own coffee, scowled at the cast on her right wrist and half her hand, and held the cup out to me without speaking. I set my own cup on the bench between us, opened hers, and handed it back.

Mutual agreement.

Dawson leaned back with a sigh, and I glanced back toward the hotel she and I had both come from. It was a giant step up from the motel—and not just because that lay in smouldering ruins—but Dawson had decreed that we deserved a bit of luxury after all we'd been through. Despite my precarious finances, I hadn't disagreed. Hot baths, comfortable beds, and twenty-four-hour security would be good for us all, I'd told myself. And I'd been right. It had been blissful. Especially the part where I felt clean for the first time in an eon.

Besides, we had more than deserved a bit of luxury by the time the hospital—and the OPP—had released us yesterday afternoon.

Explosions in the woods created a *lot* of questions, it turned out.

On the bright side, at least none of the questions had been about Rusk. There hadn't been anything left of the Mage when the police had converged on us in the woods, and they'd put their K9's interest in where he'd been standing down to the explosion itself. Dawson and I had left it at that.

"In a few days," she'd muttered to me as the paramedics assessed us, *"he'll become a missing-billionaire mystery. It's best that way."*

At least until someone came looking for him, I'd thought, but I hadn't said it.

And now we sat on the shore of Lake Ontario in the early morning sun that had risen over a world that was oblivious to all of it. To the Mages and the monsters, to the stones and the alien in their midst, and to the secret sisterhood that had sacrificed altogether too much to keep it safe. I couldn't lie. A part of me wished that I could still be oblivious, too.

I turned away from the empty stretch of grass that led to the quiet, treed street beyond and sipped my coffee as I looked back out across the water. There had been no sign of either Sister Margaret or Phoenix. Hopefully, that meant they were both still sleeping—something I hadn't done much of myself between my dreams and the unwelcome return of night-sweats that I hadn't experienced in years.

Dawson and I sat in silence for a while, each watching the world. A seagull strutted across the lawn toward us, head cocked so it could watch us with one beady eye in hopes of a handout. Disappointed, it wandered off toward the pebble beach and its companions there.

"So. An alien named Methuselah, huh?" Dawson said finally.

"And magick," I replied. "And apparently witches and Mages and disappearing monsters, too."

"You forgot the dragons."

I quirked an eyebrow at her. "Would you be surprised if they were part of this?"

"At this point?" She gave a soft snort. "Probably not."

Silence fell again, oddly comfortable. I liked Detective Sergeant Dawson, I'd decided. She was good people—not to mention a hell of an asset in this mess I'd gotten myself into. I would miss her when she returned to Toronto. Her, and Sister Margaret, and—I swallowed against a sudden lump in my throat—and Phoenix.

Holy Mother, but I'd miss Phoenix.

But a parting of the ways was for the best, I told myself firmly. I had no idea who or what might be coming after me next, or where I would be going from here, or—

As if she'd read my mind, Dawson cleared her throat. "Did you know that Sister Margaret and Phoenix were up making notes all night? They used all the hotel notepads we had in our rooms, and I think they snagged more from the lobby. They have quite a pile of them."

"Notes about what?"

"Phoenix read the journal before Rusk took it from her, and Sister Margaret has a lifetime of knowledge. They figured if they combined everything, they might find something."

The idea was a sound one, but I frowned. It seemed to me that there was a nugget of concern in what Dawson had said—aside from the nun and Phoenix wanting to remain involved, I meant—but I couldn't put my finger on it.

"And?" I prompted.

"They didn't have much when I went to bed," she said, "and I haven't seen them yet this morning, but ..."

"But what?"

"Quebec City."

"What about it?"

"Sister Margaret mentioned that it's where Methuselah disappeared from. The Ursulines were protecting him in their monastery there. I was thinking that they might know something."

I thought about it for a second, then shook my head. "Doubtful. They would have said if they had."

"What if they did, and it didn't get written down or passed on? Or it did get written down or passed on, but …" She trailed off, letting the destruction of the past few days sit between us on the bench with the drink holder.

She had a point.

"We have to start somewhere," she said quietly. "Unless you have another idea?"

I sat up straighter on the bench and turned to face her. *We*? I didn't think so. "Detective Daw—"

"Talia," she said. "Please. If we're going to Quebec City together—"

"We're not," I said, cutting her off. "We're not going anywhere together."

A tightening of her jawline told me she'd heard me, but she didn't look at me. "There is no way in hell I'm letting you do this on your own," she said after a moment. "F.Y.I."

"And there's no way in hell I'm traveling anywhere with you." I replied. "Or with Phoenix, or with Sister Margaret. Rusk was one of I don't know how many in the consortium he said had formed, and my stone is the last one they need. That makes me a target, Detective"— Dawson opened her mouth beside me to correct my use of her title, and I repeated it for good measure, with emphasis —"*Detective*, and I cannot—*will* not—be responsible for any of you getting caught in the crossfire. Or cross-explosion, or cross-magick, or whatever the hell these … Mages … throw at me."

I returned her side-eye with a flat, determined gaze of my own. "I go alone."

"And when they realize the journal is gone and Phoenix was the last one to see it?" she asked.

Fuck, I thought. *That was it. That was the nugget of concern.*

But it felt more like a boulder as it dropped into my belly.

"Or when they find out that Sister Margaret is still alive and may know things?" the detective added.

Fuck, I thought again as a second boulder joined the first. *How could I have missed that? How could I not have realized—*

"Damned if you do, damned if you don't," Dawson said softly.

I stared at her, reeling from the enormity of the truth in her words. The truth that I wasn't the only one at risk here. That we were all targets. All of us except Dawson.

A breeze off the lake ruffled my hair, and I tucked it behind my ears so that it wouldn't blow across my eyes. "You don't have to be part of this, you know," I said, partly because it was the truth but mostly because taking responsibility was just a habit with me—no nun-pun intended. "There's still time for you to go home—back to your life."

"There is," she agreed. "But I've never been to Quebec City before. It might be nice."

Nice. She thought going to Quebec City to find an alien named Methuselah—with Mages and goliaths and sweet Mary knows what else in hot pursuit—was *nice*?

"Did they check you for concussion at the hospital?" I asked, narrowing my eyes at her.

"Plus, I haven't gone on a road trip with friends in years," she added, as if I hadn't spoken.

I almost choked, but on an unexpected burble of laughter rising in my chest rather than the disbelief I should have been feeling—and then on a welling of gratitude that made my throat tighten and my eyes prickle.

Dawson wasn't in the least concussed, I realized, blinking back a haze. She was telling me—without telling me—that I wasn't alone in this. That she had my back. That she'd heard my unspoken need for help and was offering it.

Mutual agreement.

I sat back on the bench again and turned my face toward the rising sun. The breeze had untucked my hair and blown it across my eyes again, but it didn't matter. And the Mages and their monsters? Those didn't matter, either. Not in this breath, this moment, this bubble of time that held every possibility within it. Even the possibility that said a sixty-nine-year-old former nun could save the world as long as she had the right sidekicks.

"A road trip, huh?" I said. "I don't think I've ever been on one of those with anyone … Talia."

Beside me, Detective Sergeant Talia Dawson smiled. "It'll be fun," she said. "Or at least memorable. I promise."

That wrung an outright guffaw from me, startling a half dozen seagulls into flight. I laughed and laughed, and then Talia joined in, and then we both laughed some more. Because we'd survived Eldon Rusk and his monster, we were going on a road trip, and at the very least, we were going to have a memorable time.

And the most important thing, whispered a little hitch in my heart, was that despite everything I'd lost, I wouldn't be alone. I looked down at the tattooed hand holding the coffee cup Talia had given me. *No regrets* wasn't about not feeling sorrow. It was about moving on and doing the next best thing.

Most of all, it was about honoring the memories of all the women who had gone before me by standing with the ones I still had.

The Obsidian Sisterhood

The Crone Wars

Becoming Crone

A Gathering of Crones

Game of Crones

Crone Unleashed

Rise of the Crones

The Grigori Legacy

Sins of the Angels (Grigori Legacy book 1)

Sins of the Son (Grigori Legacy book 2)

Sins of the Lost (Grigori Legacy book 3)

Sins of the Warrior (Grigori Legacy book 4)

Other Books by Linda Poitevin

The Ever After Romance Collection

Gwynneth Ever After

Forever After

Forever Grace

Always and Forever

Abigail Always

Shadow of Doubt

ACKNOWLEDGEMENTS

I have a solid team behind me every time I undertake to write a new book, and I am beyond grateful to each and every one of them for their support. The ones who particularly stand out are my husband Pat, who understands my deadline insanity (and never holds it against me); my writing (and writers' retreat) buddy, Marie Bilodeau, who reminds me as often as I need to hear it that yes, I can do this; and my copy editor, Laura Paquet, who unfailingly returns a much (much) improved story to me. When I say I couldn't do this without them, I really couldn't do this without them.

Special thanks to writer friend Craig Shackleton, who let me use his *No Regrets* tattoo as the inspiration for Sister Monica's—hers isn't quite the same as his, but the intent is very much there. Thanks also to my cover designer, Deranged Doctor Design, for another stellar cover, and to beta reader Cat of Your Beta Reader, who brought fresh perspective to Monica's story where I most needed it.

And finally, special mention to my Crones Unleashed Facebook group, where the humor and magick flow as freely as the encouragement and enthusiasm. You guys truly do rock.

About the Author

Lydia M. Hawke is a pseudonym used by me, Linda Poitevin, for my urban fantasy books. Together, we are the author of books that range from supernatural suspense thrillers to contemporary romances and romantic suspense.

Originally from beautiful British Columbia, I moved to Canada's capital region of Ottawa-Gatineau more than thirty years ago with the love of my life. Which means I've been married most of my life now, and I've spent most of it here. Wow. Anyway, when I'm not plotting the world's downfall or next great love story, I'm also a wife, mom, grandma, friend, walker of a Giant Dog, keeper of many cats, and an avid gardener and food preserver. My next great ambition in life (other than writing the next book, of course) is to have an urban chicken coop. Yes, seriously… because chickens.

You can find me hanging out on Facebook at facebook.com/LydiaMHawke, and on my website at Lydia-HawkeBooks.com, where you can also join my newsletter for updates on new books (and a free story!)

I love to hear from readers and can be reached at lydia@lydiahawkebooks.com. And yes, I answer all my emails!